ROOM SERVICE

Also by Maren Stoffels

Escape Room
Fright Night

ROOM SERVICE

MAREN STOFFELS

Translated by Laura Watkinson

Underlined

Text copyright © 2021 by Maren Stoffels
Cover art copyright © 2021 by timstarkey/Getty Images;
Blood image used under license from Shutterstock.com.
Translation copyright © 2021 by Laura Watkinson

All rights reserved. Published in the United States by Underlined, an imprint of Random House Children's Books, a division of Penguin Random House LLC, New York. Originally published in paperback by Leopold, Amsterdam in 2019.

Underlined is a registered trademark and the colophon is a trademark of Penguin Random House LLC.

GetUnderlined.com

Educators and librarians, for a variety of teaching tools, visit us at RHTeachersLibrarians.com

Library of Congress Cataloging-in-Publication Data
Names: Stoffels, Maren, author. | Watkinson, Laura, translator.
Title: Room service / Maren Stoffels ; translated by Laura Watkinson.
Other titles: Room service. English.
Description: First edition. | New York : Underlined/Delacorte Press, [2021]
| Originally published in Dutch in Amsterdam by Leopold in 2019 under title:
Room service. | Audience: Ages 12 and up. | Summary: "Four friends celebrate a birthday in a luxury hotel. But what starts as a fun weekend quickly turns into an outright nightmare. They receive messages at the door of their room, revealing more and more about what exactly happened a year ago. What the messenger wants is clear: revenge"— Provided by publisher.
Identifiers: LCCN 2020029656 (print) | LCCN 2020029657 (ebook) |
ISBN 978-0-593-17598-9 (trade paperback) | ISBN 978-0-593-17599-6 (ebook)
Subjects: CYAC: Secrets—Fiction. | Revenge—Fiction. |
Mystery and detective stories.
Classification: LCC PZ7.1.S7527 Ro 2021 (print) | LCC PZ7.1.S7527 (ebook) |
DDC [Fic]—dc23

The text of this book is set in 11-point Berling LT Std.
Interior design by Andrea Lau

Printed in the United States of America
10 9 8 7 6 5 4 3 2 1
First Edition

For Vimmer, the most beautiful twist in my story

The truth and my lies now
are falling like the rain,
so let the river run

—Eminem

ROOM SERVICE

RESERVATION

≏

It's almost here.
The date I'll never forget.
It's the day they murdered her.
And it'll be the day
I murder one of them.

FENDER

She's not here.

But what was I expecting? That she'd be waiting for me, here at the harbor? Just because she wrote to me doesn't mean everything will be the same as it was before.

The letter has been burning inside my pocket all the way here. It was suddenly there on the mat this afternoon, with my name on it, in her handwriting.

I stared at it for a few seconds because I couldn't believe it was real. But in a few minutes I'll finally know what it is that she wants to tell me. I really want to read the letter here. In our special place.

I run the last few yards along the jetty.

"Hey! Good evening!"

Startled, I look around. A man is waving at me from a nearby yacht.

I wave back. If she were here now, she'd come up with a name for him. She often made up characters based on complete strangers she saw. She'd think of a name, a profession, and a home life. I always thought she might become a writer when she was older.

The man sails out of the harbor and I'm alone again. I rest my hand on the hard edge of the boat. It's upside down, propped up on poles, and the space beneath it makes the perfect hiding place. I come here every Friday, even if it's raining or stormy.

When I'm here, I can pretend, just for a while, that everything is still the same.

I crawl under the boat and take the letter from the inside pocket of my denim jacket. The envelope is a striking gold color. I hold it to my lips and breathe in deeply, hoping to pick up some of her scent.

I recognized her messy handwriting immediately. It's just as chaotic as her.

The stamp is postmarked with the name of the town where she lives now. I don't know her exact address. She doesn't want to be found—certainly not by me.

I think about my friends. If Kate and Lucas knew where I was now, they'd probably freak. They think I practice with the band every Friday evening. They have no idea that the band broke up ages ago. I left last summer, because I couldn't play anymore. I kept forgetting my solos when we were playing gigs, and my fingers wouldn't stop shaking.

I only ever use the guitar in my bedroom as something to throw my clothes over now.

My friends don't have a clue. They've both just gotten on with their lives.

Kate was broken at the time, maybe even more than I was. But after the summer break, a miracle occurred.

And that miracle was called Linnea.

Our homeroom teacher sat her next to Kate on the first day of school this year, in the one empty seat.

It was just as if Linnea had come to replace her. A new version, completely intact.

She got Kate to laugh again. I remember hearing that sound again the first day back at school and realizing it had been months since she'd last laughed.

From then on, Linnea was one of us. She came and sat with us at recess, on our bench by the river, and she'll be there this weekend when Kate celebrates her birthday.

Linnea is everywhere *she* used to be.

She patched up Kate. Lucas is crazy about her. But she can't fix me.

I open the envelope and pause for a moment.

What if this letter does even more damage? Maybe it says how much she hates me.

But then I think about the past few months. Hearing *nothing* from her is still a thousand times worse than hearing *something.*

The letter is clumsily folded in half. The paper smells of her perfume. The images that the fragrance evokes startle me.

Her body against mine.

Under this boat.

I should have soaked up those moments when I still could.

My hands shaking, I unfold the letter. But as soon as I read the first two sentences, I wish I hadn't.

There are times when hearing *something* is worse than hearing *nothing*.

I never expected to write this, but I can't go on any longer.
This is my suicide note.

LINNEA

"Tomorrow's the big day." Lucas is sitting in our usual spot by the river, staring at the opposite bank, where the setting sun is casting a pink glow over the Riverside Hotel.

I never thought I'd go inside that five-star hotel, but Kate is celebrating her birthday there tomorrow.

"Two rooms." Kate looks at us. "Far away from my dad and the people from his firm."

Kate's dad has a business meeting at the Riverside this weekend and managed to score a couple extra rooms for his daughter. There should normally be one adult per room, but no one's going to check. Besides, Kate's dad will be around if anything goes wrong.

"Two rooms? Perfect!" Lucas grins. "So I'm sharing with Linnea?"

"You wish." By now I'm so used to Lucas making remarks like this that I just fire straight back at him. "You snore."

"Do not!"

"Do too," says Kate. "Fender says he didn't sleep a wink at camp because of you."

"Hey, where *is* Fender, anyway?"

"Practicing with the band again, of course." Kate's face clouds over. I know she doesn't like it that he doesn't hang out with us much but, to be honest, it's fine by me.

The intense way Fender stares at me with those brown eyes—it gives me the shivers. Whenever I have an opinion about something, Fender automatically has to say the opposite. I constantly have to defend myself when he's around.

Lucas looks back at the opposite bank. "Just as long as he's there tomorrow, right?"

I lean over the handlebars of my racing bike and speed up. It's late, but we got to talking about the Riverside and I lost track of the time.

I'm so curious to see inside the fancy five-star hotel, with the huge glass dome above the pool. Apparently you can see the stars through it when you're swimming on your back.

As I ride my bike past the park, I hesitate for a moment, but it's by far the shortest route home, so I turn right anyway.

The lampposts shoot past and my bike light swings to and fro.

There's something eerie about the park in the darkness. The trees tower above, like huge creatures with long arms.

Behind me, I hear a rattling sound coming closer and closer. Another cyclist?

I look back, straight into the bright front light of a dark

bike. It's so big that it's more like a car's headlight. Why won't they just pass me? There's plenty of room!

I cycle a bit more to the right, but they're still panting down the back of my neck.

"Go past," I shout over my shoulder, but there's no reaction.

I feel my heart pounding. What does this person want from me? Are they some kind of creep?

I should have taken a different route!

I cycle faster, but the distance between us doesn't increase. In fact, I think it gets smaller.

I lean a bit more forward and go even faster. I'm really quick on my racing bike. I can get to school in just a few minutes.

The rattling behind me is farther away now. I keep pedaling until I think I can't hear anything.

Cautiously, I look back and then heave a sigh of relief. The bright light is gone. I've lost them!

I want to get home as quickly as possible.

But then I see a branch lying in my path. Just in time, I turn left, but I start swerving dangerously. My bike tips and I hit the asphalt with a bang, the handlebar grazing my ribs.

"Ow!" I grab the place where it hurts. For a moment, I lie there, but then I realize that the cyclist could catch up with me at any second. I scramble awkwardly to my feet, clutching my right side.

"Hello?"

Here he comes! What does this maniac want from me? You sometimes read stories about girls who . . . I'm about to pick my bike up off the ground when he shouts again.

"Linnea?"

How does he know my name? But then I realize who I was running away from.

"Fender?"

A wave of relief washes through me. Why didn't Fender just say it was him?

Maybe he was trying to scare me on purpose so he can tell everyone this weekend about how fast I tried to escape.

Fender brakes right in front of me and pulls my bike off the ground in one movement.

"What happened?" he asks.

I point at the branch. "I fell."

"Klutz."

Well, whose fault was that?

That's what I want to say to him, but as always I swallow my words. Whenever I'm with Fender, my stomach is full of words.

"What are you doing here?"

"I was just at our bench."

Fender shakes his head. "Dumb route to take."

I pretend not to hear him and get onto my bike. My ribs are hurting but I just want to get home as soon as I can.

As we ride our bikes out of the park, there's an awkward silence. There always is when it's the two of us. We simply don't have anything to say to each other. When we have to work in pairs at school, Fender always makes sure to quickly join up with Kate or Lucas before the two of us are left over.

"How did it go tonight?" I say, trying to break the silence.

"What?"

"You were just at your band practice, weren't you?"

"Oh, yeah. Great."

"So what kind of stuff are you playing now?"

"Huh?"

What is wrong with Fender? It's like his mind is somewhere else entirely.

"What are you playing now?" I repeat.

"You wouldn't know it anyway."

"How do you know?"

"I just do."

Arrogant jerk.

I glance over at him. Fender is leaning forward on his bike. A few strands of his long hair have slipped out of his bun and are hanging in front of his eyes. He has two earrings in his right ear. It's like they forgot his left ear and over-compensated on his right ear instead.

"Hey, are you actually named after the guitars?"

"No. My parents just called me Fender because they liked the meaning."

"What does it mean?"

"You know, 'protector.' Like 'defender.' "

"Yeah, that's a nice meaning. *Linnea* means 'lime tree.' "

Why did I say that? Fender stays meaningfully silent, like he really doesn't care.

It's just as well he has to go a different way soon, because I don't want to cycle next to him for even one more minute. It's like I'm riding my bike next to a complete stranger. The silence between us is worse than ever.

Why is he like that? I've never felt this way with Kate and Lucas. Not even when I'd known them just a few days.

The bike path narrows toward the exit, and Fender lets me go ahead. This part of the park is pitch black and I focus on my front light.

"I can hardly see anything."

"At least you've got a light," I hear from behind me.

It takes a moment to sink in, but then I swing around to look. My bike swerves.

"Hey, be careful! Or I'm going to have to pick you up off the ground again."

Fender's sarcastic tone barely gets through to me this time. That big headlight, the one that was just dazzling me, is nowhere to be seen.

Whoever was following me had a different bike.

It wasn't Fender.

I looked like a crazy person,
cycling that close behind her.
What if she'd seen me?
And what was *he* suddenly doing there?
I wonder if he's read the letter yet.
I put it in the mail yesterday,
right in time for the weekend.
And did he cry when he read it,
like I did?

ENTRANCE

LINNEA

"Hey, missy! You daydreaming?" A man behind me rings his bell impatiently. "The light's green!"

Startled, I ride off as quickly as I can. My ribs still feel a bit sore after falling off my bike last night.

It took me a long time to get to sleep. The thought of the bike with the big headlight kept me awake.

Who was it? What did they want? And what would have happened if Fender hadn't come along?

At the last stoplight before the Riverside, I have to wait again. The bike path is busy. There's a bunch of tourists on rental bikes, all clumped together. When the light turns green, they set off at once. I almost lose my balance as they force me up against the curb.

In a flash, I see a dark-brown bike among the other bikes. It has a big front light, like a car's headlight.

My body reacts faster than my mind does. It feels as if I'm falling, my heart skipping a beat.

He's here again.

That's not possible. Is it?

I look again, but I don't see him anywhere. The cyclist has vanished into thin air.

⸻

"Hey!" Kate squeals excitedly when I get to the Riverside. "You're the first one here."

I give her a kiss on the cheek. "Happy birthday."

I have to forget about the cyclist. I'm probably just mistaken anyway. Why would anyone want to follow me? Besides, this town's huge. There must be plenty of dark bikes with big headlights like that.

"What are you thinking about, Spinner?"

"Spinner?"

"Yeah," says Kate. "Your head always seems to be busy spinning yarns."

I feel my cheeks burning. Should I tell Kate about the cyclist? I take a deep breath, but then Kate's expression freezes. She's looking at something behind me, and when I turn around, I see Lucas approaching. He's carrying an enormous bear.

Kate sighs. "That's not for me, is it?"

I laugh. "I'm afraid so."

Lucas always gives such weird gifts. Last winter he gave me a coupon for an all-you-can-eat spare ribs restaurant, even though I've been a vegetarian for years.

"Happy birthday!" Lucas holds out the bear to Kate. "So you're not lonely at night."

"You shouldn't have." Kate makes a face. The bear is almost as big as she is.

"Where's Fender?"

"He's on his way." Kate looks down the street, fiddling nervously with her shirt. Is she really afraid he's not going to show?

But then I see Fender. As always, he's wearing a casually unbuttoned shirt with his usual denim jacket on top of it. His face looks gray, like he hasn't slept for days.

"The gang's all here!" shouts Lucas.

"Happy birthday," says Fender, kissing Kate on the cheek. I raise my hand halfway but then let it fall. He completely ignores me, as if I'm made of air.

"Now we can finally head inside!" Lucas puts an arm around Fender, and they walk to the entrance.

Kate slings the bear over her shoulder and hooks her arm through mine.

"Shall we?"

At the entrance to the Riverside, there's a doorman wearing a top hat and a uniform. I see him glance at the bear, but he keeps a straight face. He swings the door open for us, and we step into the hotel.

Sure, I knew the Riverside would be fancy, but I could never have imagined this.

In the middle of the lobby, a gigantic chandelier is suspended from the high ceiling. There's a Persian carpet just in front of the stairs, and there are lounge chairs beside a grand piano that's so shiny I can see all four of us reflected in it. Light fixtures like big torches hang on the columns that support the first floor.

I feel like I just walked onto a movie set. Like I'm playing the lead role in a major production.

I can't take my eyes off the gold clock above the entrance. It has all kinds of different hands indicating not just the time, but other things too. I recognize a few of the images around the edge of the clock as astrological symbols. I look for my star sign, the one that's like a V with a loop attached: Capricorn.

Lucas follows my gaze. "Cool, huh?"

"Yeah, totally."

Behind me I hear Kate telling Fender how many celebrities have played this piano.

"Are you sure you want to share a room with her?" Lucas says with a grin. "I might snore, but she'll keep you up all night with her chattering."

"You have a point." I smile. "I'll think about it."

Kate walks over to us with two keys in her hand. They're the old-fashioned kind, on big keychains. Most hotels use keycards these days, but everything about the Riverside is traditional.

"Got the keys! Are you coming? We need to go to the top floor."

My stomach flips when Kate walks to the elevator.

"I . . . I'll take the stairs," I say quickly.

"The stairs?" Lucas looks at me in surprise. "Why would you want to do that?"

"It keeps me fit. Anyway, the five of us will never fit inside that elevator."

"Five?"

"Us and the bear."

Lucas and Kate laugh, but Fender just raises his eyebrows. His gaze moves away from my eyes and down. The way he looks at me . . .

I can feel the blood rushing in my ears. Why do I let him get to me like that?

As I walk to the stairs, I glance at the exit. What I really want to do is run outside.

How am I going to survive a whole weekend with Fender?

But he'll still be here after this weekend too. He's at school every day, in every class, during every break. As long as I hang out with Kate and Lucas, I'll get Fender thrown in for free.

When I turn around, Kate gives me a little wave. She looks radiant, as if she's giving off light.

I can't leave. She's so happy we're all here. I think she really was afraid Fender wouldn't show.

If I go now, I'll spoil her birthday weekend, and she doesn't deserve that. She was there for me on my very first day at school, and now I have to be here for her.

I turn onto the stairs, but then I bump into someone, really hard. It's so painful that my eyes fill with tears, and I stand there, rubbing my shoulder.

Then I look back, but to my surprise no one's there. Whoever it was just went on walking.

***

"I'll let you do the honors." Kate hands me our key and steps aside. I can already hear Lucas's enthusiasm all the way from the boys' room.

My heart is pounding as I turn the key in the lock. It's like I'm a kid again and unwrapping a big present.

As the door opens, I actually feel my jaw drop. The room has a golden glow, which almost hurts my eyes. Cream-colored carpet covers the floor, and there are paintings of historical hunting scenes on the walls.

I'm surprised to see a tray on the coffee table with two glasses on it. Beside it is a bottle of champagne in a cooler. The hotel clearly thinks all the rooms will have adult occupants.

There's even a separate work area with a mahogany desk and two deep leather chairs.

But the most amazing thing about the room is the gigantic four-poster bed, with its silk curtains and dozens of cushions in all shapes and sizes.

When I turn around, I see that Kate isn't looking at the room. She's looking at me. Her eyes are gleaming.

"You up for it?"

Before I can ask what she means, Kate runs and jumps onto the bed. The comforter flies up as she lands, and then it slowly descends. Kate lies facedown in one of the pillows and mumbles something unintelligible.

"How was it?"

"This is something you need to experience for yourself, Spinner," Kate replies. "There are no words to describe it."

I take a run-up and fly onto the bed, landing next to Kate. My ribs are still painful, but the soft mattress makes everything okay. I sink so deep into it that it feels like I'll never be able to stand up again. We roll onto our backs and gaze up at the ceiling with its spotlights. It's like lying under a starry sky.

"I don't know if I can sleep in here," I say. "Seems a shame to close your eyes."

Kate grins. "After we've finished that bottle of champagne, you'll be able to sleep. Oh, and the boys have a bottle too."

My thoughts immediately return to Fender, and the bad feeling is back again.

"What are you thinking about?" Kate sits up and grabs my hair.

I can feel her braiding my hair behind my back. She's really skilled and quick.

"I was thinking about Fender," I blurt out.

"Fender? How come?"

I can't be honest with her. She'll never understand.

"You've known each other a long time, haven't you?"

"Our whole lives. Our moms went to mother-to-be yoga classes together," Kate says with a smile. "That's why we're both so zen."

If there's one person I know who's incapable of sitting still, it's Kate.

"What do you like best about him?"

Maybe I need to hear it from someone else. Maybe then I'll finally see Fender in a different light.

"The way he's so musical," says Kate without having to think about it. "When he's playing, it's like nothing else exists for a moment. Fender is so different from Lucas, much more thoughtful. Sometimes you can almost literally hear him thinking. He's just different from all the other guys I know."

I think about Fender's dark eyes. When I'm with him, it feels like I'm standing in line for a terrifying roller coaster. Yeah, he certainly is different.

Kate takes a hair tie off her wrist and puts the braid over my shoulder. "Done."

"I never wear my hair in a braid."

"It suits you, though." Kate nods approvingly. "So what do *you* think of Fender?"

I feel myself blushing. If I lie now, she's going to notice.

So all I say is "I . . . I sometimes have the feeling he's not doing that great."

Kate's face clouds over. "What do you mean?"

"Don't you think he looks kind of bad?"

"Yeah . . . ," Kate says, fiddling with the ring on her pinky finger. It's a child's ring with a silver four-leaf clover on it.

"And yesterday evening I bumped into him in the park and he seemed pretty . . . preoccupied," I say.

"I know what you mean." Kate slides off the bed. "I'll have a word with him."

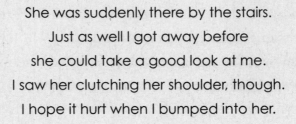

She was suddenly there by the stairs.
Just as well I got away before
she could take a good look at me.
I saw her clutching her shoulder, though.
I hope it hurt when I bumped into her.

FENDER

She's dead.

How can she be dead and I didn't even realize?

I drum my fingers on the windowsill. From here I have a beautiful view out across the river to the houses opposite, but I don't care. I couldn't care less about this whole hotel.

How am I supposed to celebrate Kate's birthday this weekend when she's . . . But maybe it's not true. Maybe she just wanted to give me a scare.

I reach into the inside pocket of my denim jacket. The gold envelope is still there.

I've read the words more times than I wanted to, but I couldn't help it. They stabbed me like knives, over and over, but in a weird way it felt good. I deserve the punishment. The words are carved into me so I'll never forget them.

At first I thought Kate and Lucas had received letters too, but when I met them at the entrance, I could tell at once that I was the only one.

What if it's really true? What if she really did commit suicide because of what happened last year?

A wave of nausea hits me.

"Fender?" Lucas looks at me. "I asked you a question."

"What?"

"Do you want to come for a swim?"

Lucas points at his swim briefs, which he's already put on. Typical Lucas. He's not bothered that he's at a five-star hotel, where that sort of thing is completely inappropriate.

His bare legs look tanned under the bright-yellow fabric. Next to him, I feel like a milk bottle. She always used to tease me about it, to the point where it got irritating. Now I'd give anything if she'd tease me again, just one more time.

It can't be true, can it? That she's gone? I'd have felt something like that.

"No, go without me," I say. I can't go swimming with them, pretending to be happy, when I feel like this. I'm sure Kate will realize immediately that something's up—and then the questions will start.

What am I supposed to say to her? That the girl who used to be her best friend has committed suicide? Kate will break all over again, into a thousand pieces. I can't do that to her.

"Huh? Why aren't you coming?"

"Swollen toe." I shrug. "Sucks."

"Are you kidding me? Now of all times!" Lucas flashes me a look of irritation. "Can't you put a plastic bag over it or something?"

"Nope. Doctor's orders."

"Awesome." Lucas stuffs a towel into his bag.

I look outside again. A boat full of tourists is sailing along the river.

"Are you guys ready?" I hear Kate ask.

"Fender's not coming. Something about a swollen toe."

"What a bunch of crap!" Kate looks at me. "You can just sit on the side, can't you?"

I want them to go away. I need to be alone. I have to read the letter again.

"You guys go," I say. "I'll see you later."

"But . . ."

"No, it's not happening, Kate."

There's a moment's silence. I bet Kate's going to give it another try. She can be really insistent when she doesn't get her way. She's always been like that.

"Hey, where's your guitar?" she says then.

I feel the hairs rise on the back of my neck. "What do you mean?"

Kate looks around the room. "You always bring it to parties, so why not this time?"

"I . . . I forgot it."

"Forgot it?" Kate shakes her head. She doesn't believe me. Of course she doesn't. I used to drag that thing around with me everywhere. No one ever needed to put on music. I was the jukebox. I could play everything. My fingers knew every request.

Kate and Lucas danced, and *she* listened. With her head

in her hands, and a dreamy look in her eyes. She was the reason I played until my fingers cramped up.

"But what about my birthday present?" Kate says. "You always give me a song every year!"

I should have known she'd bring that up. The tradition began when Kate said she already has everything. So every year I'd write a song and play it specially for her.

But how can I play guitar now that *she* isn't here anymore? I haven't touched my guitar for almost a year now.

"Fender can play without a guitar."

All three of us look up in surprise. Linnea is standing in the doorway, blushing a bit.

"Can't you?"

"What do you mean?" asks Lucas.

"Well, he practices every day during classes. He mutters the lyrics and drums under his chair with his fingers."

Linnea's words slowly shatter inside my head. Until now, only one person ever noticed that. It was something between the two of us. Even Kate had never spotted my tic.

When I'm nervous, I practice solos and I hear the tune in my head. It makes me feel calm.

Why would Linnea of all people notice that?

"Is that true?" Kate asks me. She bursts out laughing. "Weirdo!"

"Of course it's not," I say loudly. "She doesn't know what she's talking about. Linnea sees things that aren't there."

I look at Linnea, who is hanging her head. What's she

doing here anyway? *She* should have been here. We'd have shared a room at the Riverside and we'd have made fun of the luxury.

We were already making plans for after high school. The four of us were going to study in the same city.

How can everything change in just one moment?

I *hate* Linnea, with her innocent blue eyes. She has no idea whose place it is that she was so eager to take.

"Come on, let's go to the pool," says Lucas, pulling Linnea along with him. As they head down the hallway, Kate gives me a searching look.

Is she going to say something else about my guitar? I know that look on her face. She's not letting it go.

But I force myself to look back at her until my eyes start to water.

Kate is the first to turn away and, without saying anything, she closes the door behind her.

I look at myself in the mirror above the bathroom sink. The skin under my eyes is thin and purple, and my cheeks are sunken.

I look like some kind of junkie. My friends must have noticed too.

I feel like I might collapse of exhaustion at any minute, and also like I'll never be able to sleep again.

I'm way too scared of the nightmares.

Her inside a casket.

Arms crossed and eyes shut.

Did she suffer?

How did she do it?

Pills? Jumping? A noose?

I press my fingertips to my temples. My head is exploding with questions.

Then, suddenly, there are three loud knocks on the door. Startled, I look back. Could Lucas have forgotten something?

"Room service," says a muffled voice.

Did Lucas order some food? He eats all day long but never puts on an ounce.

I rub my cheeks and walk to the door. When I open it, I'm surprised to see no one there.

Then I spot the stainless-steel dome at my feet. It's a cloche, one of those things that hotels use to cover food.

I can't imagine Lucas would have gone ahead and ordered a meal. Not here. The prices at this place are insane. Even a simple salad costs a fortune.

It was probably just delivered to the wrong room.

For a moment, I consider ignoring it and shutting the door, but my rumbling stomach stops me.

A bite to eat—that's probably not a bad idea. I barely had anything for breakfast, and lunch was just a slice of toast.

So what's under the dome? I'm hoping for a burger and fries.

Just the thought of it makes my mouth water.

I lift the cloche, but there's no food under it. Just an envelope grinning up at me from the plate.

A gold envelope.

Like the one in my pocket.

With my name on it.

Blood buzzes through my head like a swarm of bees.

Is it a coincidence?

I look left and right down the hallway, but there's no one around.

I stoop and take the envelope from the plate. My fingers shaking, I tear it open.

There's a newspaper clipping inside, with today's date on it.

Suddenly the sky turned black,
and we sailed in stormy weather.
Our sun went out, but her glorious light
will warm our hearts forever.
Isolde Lieve Veerman
Daughter of Tom and Jeannette
Sister of Marius

I stare at the date of her death in the newspaper.

She's been gone a few days now.

It's real.

I pull the plate and silver dome into the room and close

the door behind me. My heart pounds as I read the words over and over again.

I stare at the names of her family.

Tom, Jeannette, and Marius.

I spent so much time at their place that they felt a bit like my own family.

In the mornings, I was often alone with her dad. Tom was the only early bird in the family, until I started sleeping over on the weekends.

He liked me.

And now his daughter is dead.

Because of me.

I reach for the letter in my inside pocket. Her family must never read these words.

They'd kill us.

But wait a second . . .

I didn't receive the letter until yesterday.

By which time she had already been dead a few days.

So when did she send the letter?

But then I see the small letters on the back of the newspaper clipping. They're written in blue ink, in overly neat handwriting.

Now she really is dead.
But you guys killed her already,
364 days ago.

Too bad I had to run away so quickly.
I'd have loved to see your reaction.

LINNEA

*She doesn't know what she's talking about. Linnea sees
things that aren't there.*

How can Fender say things like that? Why didn't I stand
up to him?

He made me out to be some kind of fantasist.

I walk to the hot tub, which is all the way at the back of
the room. Kate and Lucas jumped right into the pool, but I
want to be alone for a while. The hot tub is the perfect place,
hidden behind tropical plants.

I go down the steps into the hot tub and lower myself
into the water. The bubbles aren't on, but I enjoy the warm
water.

Why do I let that guy get to me? I know what I saw.
Fender really does have a tic.

Behind me, I hear a scraping sound, like someone just
bumped into a lounger.

"Lucas?" When I turn around, I don't see anyone. "Kate?"

No reaction.

Then the bubbles start and my voice disappears into
the noise.

I lie back and close my eyes, breathing in deep the scent of lavender.

I'm not going to let Fender ruin my weekend. The Riverside is a place I've always wanted to go, and I'd like to enjoy it one hundred percent. I'll just ignore him for the rest of the weekend if I have to. After all, that's what he does to me.

The bubbles are soothing. Briefly, the thought of Fender fades into the background. This is such a luxury. I'd love to stay in here all weekend.

But then I get this weird tingling sensation on the back of my head. It's exactly the same feeling I had in the park and at the stoplight. The feeling that I'm being watched . . .

"Lucas? Kate?"

I stand up and climb out of the hot tub. The wet tiles feel cold under my bare feet. My braid drips down my back.

"Guys," I shout, much louder now. I feel vulnerable in my wet bikini.

I see a shadow dart away by the lounge chairs.

"Very funny, Lucas," I call. "But I saw you. The joke's over."

Then there's a clattering sound. What was that? The door to the changing rooms is swinging back and forth, like someone just ran through them.

"What are you shouting about?"

I spin around and find myself looking into the faces of Kate and Lucas.

"Something wrong?"

It wasn't Lucas. Can't have been. He's coming from a completely different direction.

The image of the bike with the big headlight flashes into my mind. What if I was right about what I saw at the stoplight?

Linnea sees things that aren't there.

I look at the door again. There *was* a shadow. I'm sure there was. And whoever it was ran away, like they were afraid I'd see them.

"No, it's nothing," I say quickly, with a forced smile. "Let's go have a drink."

It's about time for me to introduce myself to her.

BAR

FENDER

But you guys killed her already, 364 days ago.

The words make me feel like my throat's squeezing shut.

The pattern on the wallpaper ripples, like the road surface on a hot day.

I run to the window, which I can hardly manage to get open. As the breeze hits my face, I suck in the fresh air.

Who wrote that?

And why?

Do they want to punish us for what happened last year?

The questions jostle around inside my head like a crowd at a concert.

It has to be someone who knew her. Whoever it was, they sent the letter to my address.

And that someone is in this hotel.

Marius?

I try to picture her brother, but he was always a bit slow. Her complete opposite.

Her parents, then?

No. Tom would turn up on my doorstep and tell me how disgusted he was with me.

But I can't see him sneaking about like this.

I take another look at the neat handwriting. What kind of person writes like that? Could it be a friend from where she lives now? Maybe a new boyfriend?

The idea that there might have been another guy after me makes me nauseous.

I should never have let her go.

I hear voices out in the hallway—and they're coming closer. It takes a second, but then I recognize them. It's Kate and Lucas. They're back!

I slam the window and stuff the newspaper clipping into my jeans pocket. I hear the sound of the key in the door as I run to the bed and drop onto the mattress. Just in time.

Kate and Lucas come in, closely followed by Linnea.

"What happened here?" Lucas gapes as he looks around the room.

I suddenly see the room through his eyes. The curtain is bundled up on the windowsill, the champagne glasses have fallen over, and the silver dome is lying on the floor, upside down, with the empty plate beside it.

"Did you order room service?" Kate asks, surprised.

I shake my head, barely able to speak. "Delivered to the wrong room."

"But you ate it anyway?"

I nod. My throat is locked. The gold envelope is just sticking out under the heater. I try with all my might not to look at it.

46

"We came to fetch you to go to the bar. We want a drink."
Lucas looks at me. "Can you handle a drink with that toe of
yours?"

I know he's mad at me for leaving him alone with the
girls. Lucas often grumbles when I cycle away after school
on Fridays. I say it's for the band, but of course I'm off to the
harbor.

"I'll cope," I say in a strained voice.

"Great." Kate turns around to Lucas and Linnea. "You
two go ahead. I just want to ask Fender something. Oh, and
put it on the Zuidervanck tab—my dad's paying."

"Cool!" Without asking any more questions, Lucas drags
Linnea away. For the second time, I'm left behind with Kate,
who sits on the edge of the bed.

I feel my armpits sweating when she looks at me again.

"Okay, I'm done with this. You're acting weird."

I was right: she's on to me. It's not all advantages, knowing each other for so long.

"I know this weekend is tough, but we have to get
through it."

Kate has no idea how far she is from the truth. Of course,
it was exactly a year ago, but that's not the problem anymore.

The problem is in my jeans pocket.

"Listen." Kate puts her hand on my arm. I look at the
ring with the four-leaf clover on her pinky finger. It was their
friendship ring. They both had the same one. They won them

47

at the carnival. It was a kids' prize, so it won't fit around any other finger.

"I miss her too, Fender."

She has no idea. . . . What would she do if I told her?

I try to picture Kate as she was before Linnea came along. Broken. Do I want that Kate to come back?

"We have to move on, Fender. She's not here anymore."

Kate doesn't know just how very true those words are. *You're right!* I want to scream. *She's not here. She's dead!*

But instead I pull my arm away. I have to find out who sent us this message. Maybe I can solve it without involving Kate and Lucas. I need to figure out what this person wants from us.

"We have to keep moving on." It's a struggle to speak each of the words. "And that's why we're going to the bar now."

Making a huge effort, I haul myself to my feet and hold out my hand.

As Kate stands up, the image of the hospital shoots into my mind. Exactly a year ago tomorrow night.

We faced each other by the coffee machine then, just as we're doing now.

So many moments have vanished from my memory, but that one is crystal clear. Kate didn't say anything. She did exactly what I needed.

She held me tight.

I didn't know where my body stopped and hers began.

She was my life preserver. Without her, I would have drowned.

"I'm so glad you're here this weekend." Kate's eyes glisten as she looks at me. "I can imagine how difficult this must be for you."

Before I can answer, she puts her arms around me again. This hug feels very different from then, because now I know something Kate doesn't.

Before, it felt like she was dead, but now that she really is, I can feel the difference. The empty place inside my chest has hollowed out even more, as if I'm just a thin shell.

"Of course I'm here," I mumble, freeing myself from her embrace.

LINNEA

A couple of lovebirds by the window, an elderly man right beside us, the barman himself . . .

Could one of them be my stalker? Would I recognize them if they were standing right in front of me?

"What's up with you?" asks Lucas.

I look at him. "What do you mean?"

"You keep peering around, like you're looking for someone."

Linnea sees things that aren't there.

If I tell him about my stalker now, Lucas might not take me seriously. When I think about it, it sounds kind of like a childish fantasy.

Who would want to stalk me?

Besides, I have no proof at all, just a shadow I saw darting away.

"I was just looking at the hotel," I quickly lie. "The Riverside is so fancy."

I have to let it go. This is pointless. What good will it do me to drive myself crazy?

"I was a bit disappointed there's no champagne coming out of the bathroom faucets."

I smile. "Yeah, that's a bummer."

"You're smiling again," Lucas says with a grin. "It suits you better."

I clink my glass of soda against his. "To the Riverside, then?"

"To the Riverside." Lucas takes a drink and then lowers his glass. "You want to go swimming tonight? Just you and me."

I look at him in surprise. "Tonight?"

"We have to see that starry sky, don't we?"

There's no way I'd go back to that place alone, certainly not in the dark, but with Lucas around I'll be safe. If I do have a stalker, he won't do anything if Lucas is there.

"It's a good plan, isn't it? Then you'll be rid of Fender for a while too."

I almost choke on my soda.

"Hey, I'm not blind," Lucas says with a smile. "You don't like Fender."

How does he know that? It's obvious that Fender doesn't like *me*, but the other way around? I push down the ice cube in my soda with my index finger and let it bob back up.

"Hey, it doesn't matter." Lucas gives me a nudge. "I know Fender can be insensitive."

"Really?" I ask tentatively. This doesn't feel safe at all. "But he's your best friend."

"Yeah, and?" Lucas takes another drink. "Even best friends

want to kill each other sometimes, don't they? I'm sure it's the same with you and Kate."

I think about the times when Kate acts so spoiled. When I bought a birthday gift for her, I was so nervous. What do you buy for someone who has everything? The necklace is still in my bag. I keep putting off the moment when I'm going to give it to her.

"That's true," I say.

"Fender doesn't let many people in. It's nothing personal. You just need to give him a bit of time."

"I've known him for nine months," I say.

Lucas laughs. "Okay. A bit more time, then."

Could Lucas be right? I can hardly imagine that he is.

"You won't tell Kate, will you?"

Lucas looks at me. "Of course not. Kate thinks we're all best friends forever."

"Thank you."

Lucas nods. "No problem. So are you coming swimming later?"

I push the fear of my stalker into the background.

"Okay. But right now I'm going to pee. All this soda and talk about swimming is having an effect."

When I head to the bathroom, I see a boy standing at the candy machine. He's slapping it and cursing.

"Something stuck?" I ask.

The boy turns around, looking sheepish.

"Sorry, I . . ."

"I've been there." I walk over to him and see a candy bar stuck in one of the rings. "That's what you're after, right?"

"Yes." The boy smiles apologetically. "Sorry, I don't normally get that mad, but when it comes to food . . ."

"How about I give it a try?"

Without waiting for his answer, I squeeze my arm into the opening behind the flap.

"That won't help. I already tried and . . ."

There's a dull thud, and I produce the bar.

"How did you do that?" His eyes widen. "I've been trying without success for fifteen minutes!"

"That's my little secret." I stand up. "Enjoy the candy."

"Thanks." The boy unwraps the bar and breaks off half of it. "Want some?"

"Nice." I take the candy.

Then the thought that he could be my stalker shoots through my head. But it disappears as quickly as it came. There's nothing scary about him. He's even a bit average, a real boy next door. He looks kind of casual, with his messy hair, and his eyes are friendly as he looks at me through his round glasses.

"Hi. I'm Linnea." I hold out my hand. He gives it a firm shake.

"Claus." He makes a face. "They named me after my grandpa. Terrible, isn't it?"

I shake my head. "No, it's a nice name."

"You just feel sorry for me. I can tell."

I snort with laughter. "No, no, honestly!"

"Well, here's to you and your candy-machine skills." Claus bumps my half of the chocolate bar with his. "Cheers."

We both take a bite.

"Are you here with your mom and dad too?" Claus makes a bored face. "Mine are here for work."

"They don't work for Zuidervanck, do they?"

Claus nods. "Yeah, the law firm."

So his parents work with Kate's dad. Maybe Kate knows him.

"I'm friends with his daughter, Kate," I say. "We're here to celebrate her birthday."

"Very fancy." Claus whistles. "How big is the party?"

"Oh, just four of us. I think Kate's dad got a discount," I say, feeling the need to defend myself. "We have two rooms. Kate and I are sharing, and the boys, Lucas and Fender, are in the other room. We're all in the same class at school."

Claus swallows the last bite of the candy bar. "What about that other girl?"

"Huh? Which other girl?"

"That . . . Isabel? No, that wasn't it. Isolde?"

I pause to think. "No . . . It doesn't ring any bells."

Claus frowns. "I'm pretty sure that's what she was called."

What's he talking about?

"There was this drinks party for the law firm, and the kids were allowed to go. Someone introduced me to Frank's daughter, who was hanging out with her friends there. I thought there was another blond girl with them. She was dating one of the boys."

An ex? Of Lucas or Fender? Why have I never heard them mention her? She must have been Fender's girlfriend, because Lucas is always going on about having been single forever.

The name Isolde doesn't mean anything to me. If they'd ever mentioned it, I'd have remembered. It's not like it's a common name.

"Hey, I could be wrong," Claus adds quickly.

"When was this drinks party?"

Claus thinks about it. "Last year, around this time, I think."

Only a year ago? So that was just before I came along. Why did no one ever tell me anything about this Isolde?

"Cool that you're here with your friends, though." Claus sounds jealous. "It's better than sitting by yourself in a room all weekend."

I just nod. Something about this story isn't right. All kinds of alarm bells are going off in my stomach.

Claus raises his hand. "Sorry, got to get going. Thanks for the help, Linnea. If my candy ever gets stuck again, I'll come find you."

"Ah, there you are." Lucas pushes my stool back. "You were gone for ages."

"I got to talking with someone." It's only now that I realize I completely forgot to go to the bathroom. "Where are Fender and Kate?"

"No idea." Lucas sighs. "Great birthday, huh?"

"Was it more fun last year?" I blurt out.

Lucas looks up in surprise. His cheeks are red.

"Last year?" he echoes.

"When Isolde was still around?"

There is a brief silence.

"Isolde? I don't know anyone called Isolde." Lucas takes a swig of his drink and points behind me. "Hey, there they are. Finally."

The blush on his cheeks has disappeared, as if someone erased it.

Kate and Lucas start talking about dinner, which is supposed to be fabulous at the Riverside. Kate looks flushed, as if she's been arguing, but no one mentions it.

Fender hauls himself up onto the barstool, like it's a mountain he has to climb. As always, he doesn't deem me worthy of a glance.

You are such an incredible jerk.

Why did that Isolde ever like him? I can't imagine anyone wanting Fender as a boyfriend.

Maybe that Claus guy was lying, but why would he do that? And Lucas reacted really strangely too. I've never seen him blush before. Seems like the subject of Isolde is off-limits.

Then Fender stands up and leaves the bar.

"Where's he off to?"

"Probably off for a smoke." Lucas shakes his head. "It took him months to quit. Loser."

Without thinking about it, I jump down from my stool too.

"Where are you going?" Lucas calls after me, but I don't reply. For the first time ever, I actually want to be alone with Fender. Lucas can deny knowing Isolde, but something tells me I'll have more success with Fender.

The housekeeper's master key
was just lying on her cart.
People are so careless.
Now I can go wherever I like.

FENDER

I had to get out of the bar with that irritating jazz music. The singer's warbling was really setting me on edge.

Outside I bum a cigarette and a light off a guy walking past. As I take the first drag, I feel the tension flow out of my body.

The fog inside my mind lifts a little.

The last thing I should do is panic. I have to keep a clear head.

There's someone in the hotel who knows us, someone who knows which rooms we're staying in. He knew we'd be here this weekend, but how? Lucas has been shouting about it at every opportunity, of course—is that how Room Service found out? And he's probably been watching us since we got here. I bet he saw us go into our rooms.

How long has he been watching us?

Was he watching when I opened the letter at the harbor yesterday?

I take another drag. She never wanted to kiss me when I'd been smoking, said I tasted like an ashtray.

I shove the thought of her back into the imaginary file cabinet inside my head.

Kate and Lucas can't find out about it, but what if Room Service comes back when they're around? Plus the death notice is in today's newspaper! What if someone in our class sees it? Or a teacher?

No one has ever mentioned it at school. After the summer break, there seemed to be an unspoken agreement not to say her name. I knew people were gossiping, but the conversations always fell silent when we entered the room.

No one wanted to confront us.

What had happened was bad enough.

I take another drag and start coughing.

"Nasty habit, huh?"

I look up and, to my amazement, see Linnea standing there.

"Nope."

"It's too bad." Linnea slides her sneaker over the pavement. "Lucas just told me how hard you found it to quit."

"I can quit again," I say, acting tough, but I know she's right. Last time, nothing helped. Not nicotine patches and not chewing gum. When I finally quit, it was for her. But I don't have that motivation anymore.

"Quitting for the second time is even harder."

"What do you know about it?"

"I used to smoke too."

What? Linnea smoking? I can't picture it.

"Seriously," says Linnea. "A pack a day."

I flick the butt onto the street and then watch as the glowing tip of the cigarette slowly fades.

"So what did you actually come out here for?"

Yesterday in the park she seemed delighted when we finally got to go our separate ways.

"Just for a talk." Linnea stares ahead. She seems nervous, keeps rocking forward onto her toes.

That's the Linnea I know. Her blue eyes always look like she's being hunted. Her fidgeting is getting on my nerves. Linnea is even more irritating than jazz.

She wants to talk, so why doesn't she say something?

"Hey, great chat. Now I'm going back inside." I walk past Linnea and toward the entrance.

I have to come up with a plan to unmask Room Service. If I figure out what he wants, I can make this stop.

But then I suddenly hear Linnea's voice behind me.

"Who's Isolde?"

LINNEA

For a moment, there's silence, as if someone has paused the movie we're acting in. And then the picture suddenly speeds up to make up for the lost time.

Fender pivots and puts his hand around my throat. Shoving me against the wall, he brings his face right up to mine.

"*What* did you say?"

"I . . ." I can hardly speak. Fender's eyes are suddenly black, as if someone turned off the light.

Let go. You're scaring me.

"Answer me!"

I can't breathe, you idiot. Let go of me!

I'm gasping for breath and start coughing. Fender lets go and takes a step back, as if I'm infected with something.

"Hey, you!" The doorman comes running toward us and grabs hold of Fender. "What's going on here?"

I touch the painful place on my throat. It's like Fender's fingers still have hold of me.

What just happened? Why did he flip out like that?

"Think you're a tough guy, young man?"

"I'm sorry," Fender quickly says. "I didn't know what I was doing."

You did know. You just completely snapped.

"That's pretty obvious!" The doorman looks at me. "Are you okay?"

No, of course I'm not.

"Yes, I'm fine. We . . . We're friends."

It hurts to talk. A bit like when I had my tonsils taken out and for days I had to write anything I wanted to say on a sheet of paper.

"Nice friend!" the doorman says, looking disapprovingly at Fender. "Do you want me to fetch someone?"

It was my question that did it. As soon as he heard Isolde's name, he flipped. I have to find out why.

"No, thanks," I say quietly. "There's no need."

Fender has fled back inside without saying anything else. The doorman is back in position by the entrance. I can still feel Fender's fingers around my throat.

He's lost his mind. The look in his eyes was so very dark. . . .

I glance over at the bikes. I want to go home. There's no way I can go back to the bar and pretend nothing happened.

Kate's sure to notice something's wrong. And what am I supposed to say?

Your best friend just tried to strangle me?

I run my eyes along the bike rack. My racing bike shines back at me.

The idea is so appealing. Away from Fender and his pitch-black eyes. I'll lie to Kate and Lucas, tell them I got sick. Stomach flu.

Then my gaze moves on—and I see it.

The bike with the big headlight, like a car's.

He's here.

I was right.

I haven't gone crazy. The bike is parked in front of the Riverside!

I walk over to it and examine the frame, as if there might be a name on it somewhere. When I touch the headlight, it's like an electric shock.

My stalker is here. He was at the stoplight and by the pool just now. He was watching me sitting there in my bikini.

I suddenly feel dirty, like he's been pawing me.

I turn and go back inside the hotel. I'm going to fetch my things and get away. I won't stay here for a minute longer than I have to.

From the lobby, I take the stairs two steps at a time. I need my bike key and my bag, and then I'm out of here.

On the last step, someone passes me and I feel a hand around my wrist.

Fender . . .

"Get your hands off me!" I lash out with my free hand.

"Hey, hey, calm down."

There's a laugh and it's only then that I realize it's not Fender at all. Claus lets go of my wrist.

"It's just me."

I wipe my eyes, but they fill with tears again.

"What's wrong?" Claus says, looking at me with shock.

"Does that bike outside belong to you?"

Claus frowns. "Which bike?"

"No jokes. The brown one with the big headlight. Is it yours?"

"What are you talking about?"

"Answer me!"

Claus shakes his head. "No."

"I'm going home." I start walking, but Claus stops me again. I feel something bubbling up deep inside me—and it comes out as a scream.

"Let go of me!"

"Sorry." Claus holds up his hands. "I didn't mean to . . . I'm sorry. But what on earth is going on?"

"Nothing." But as I say it, the dam in my eyes bursts and the tears come pouring out.

Claus gently reaches out and brushes a tear from my cheek. "I can't handle it when girls cry."

I feel so ashamed, but I just can't stop crying.

"Hey, why don't you come . . ." Claus pauses. "No, never mind."

"What?" I hiccup.

Claus shakes his head. "I was going to ask if you'd like to come back to my room, but that's clearly a dumb idea."

"No." My mom would murder me if I accepted his invitation. Going to a hotel room with a complete stranger is about the dumbest thing you could do.

"Maybe you could talk to your friends about whatever it is," suggests Claus.

"My friends are the problem."

I think about Kate and Lucas, who are waiting for me in the bar. What will happen if I tell them the truth?

Kate and Fender grew up together, and Fender is Lucas's best friend.

Lucas might have been pretty sympathetic before, but I think this is a step too far. And it certainly will be when Fender twists everything so it's like I'm trying to make him look bad. Like he did when I mentioned his tic.

Linnea sees things that aren't there.

Fender has a big head start when it comes to his friends—and he knows it.

"Or I could listen to you," Claus suggests. "It would be too bad if the world's best candy-machine whisperer went home."

I hurry up the last few steps.

"Okay, I'll just go back to my mom and dad, then." Claus points at two adults who are talking farther down the hallway. The woman glances in our direction and smiles. He looks like her.

"See you, Linnea."

I watch as Claus walks toward them. He's not involved in any of this. He's the only one I could dare to confide in about Fender, without unleashing a war between my friends.

"Claus," I call after him. "Wait a minute."

Inside my head, I count the seconds.

Is this going to work?

I've almost reached the couple.

What should I do?

There's no way they're going to play along and

pretend to be my parents.

I'm bluffing and it's way too much of a risk.

But then I hear Linnea's voice.

"Claus, wait a minute."

FENDER

It was because of that question.

It was because of her name.

I haven't heard it for months, only in my own thoughts.

I slam the door of the hotel room behind me. How could I have been so stupid as to let Linnea catch a glimpse of the real Fender? The Fender who waits for the impossible to happen at the harbor every Friday. The Fender I became last year on Kate's birthday.

What is Linnea going to think now? I just left her standing there on the sidewalk!

What if she tells Kate and Lucas what happened outside? I wouldn't dare face them. . . .

How does Linnea know that name? Has Kate been talking about her? I wouldn't think so. Kate hardly ever talks about her to me, let alone anyone else.

Or Lucas? He's got a big mouth. Maybe he let something slip.

There's a knock at the door.

"Room service," comes a voice from the hallway.

I freeze. It's him.

I start moving way too late, and when I look through the peephole, I don't see anyone. He's made a quick getaway, just like the first time.

I pull the door open and see another cloche at my feet. Of course I knew there'd be another message, but somehow I still hoped the death notice would be the last one.

With a bad feeling, I lift the silver dome. There's a gold envelope underneath, just like the first two.

This time it doesn't have only my name on it, but also Kate's and Lucas's.

I take it all back into the room and slump onto the bed.

Inside the envelope is a letter, clumsily folded in half.

When I read the first sentence, the same thing happens as yesterday: everything around me stands still.

It's a copy of her letter.

> *I never expected to write this, but I can't go on any longer.*
>
> *This is my suicide note.*
>
> *You might read this and think you can still stop me, but you're too late.*
>
> *I'll make sure I'm gone by the time you read this.*
>
> *What does it matter now, anyway?*

I actually died last year on Kate's birthday.

I know that and so do they.

Kate, Fender, and Lucas.

My so-called best friends.

The night is almost over, but I can no longer

tell the difference between night and day.

It's always dark for me.

Isolde

Once again, I read the words that hurt me more and more every time. I relive every word. I breathe in every sentence.

Why is Room Service sending me this letter again? Does he want to let me know that there are copies?

But then I see the brief message on the reverse side, in that overly neat handwriting.

Show this letter to Kate and Lucas—or I will. I'll give you an hour.

This message is specially for me. He knows I'm alone. He's watching us.

I take another look at the neat handwriting, even though I know there's no point. I don't know anyone who writes like that.

Who would do this? He's giving me an hour to tell them everything, but where should I begin?

There is one loud knock at the door, and I immediately sit up.

Room Service. This time I'm going to catch him if it's the last thing I do. I leap off the bed and sprint to the door, banging my shin against the coffee table, but that doesn't stop me. I swing the door open—and I find myself looking into Lucas's surprised face.

"You okay?"

"Was that you?" I look past him and down the long hallway. "Did you just knock?"

"Yes, you've got the key."

I look down the hallway again. "Did you see anyone on your way to the room?"

Lucas frowns. "What's going on?"

"Just tell me!"

"No . . . No, I didn't see anyone. Dude, what is it? You look kind of freaked out."

I rub my throbbing shin. How much time do I have left? At least five minutes have already gone by.

"Is Fender here?" Kate peeks around the door. "Oh, there you are. Everything all right?"

"That's what I was just asking." Lucas gives me a worried look.

"Have you been taking pills or something?"

"Of course not."

"Where's Linnea?" asks Kate. "I thought she was with you."

Linnea. So they haven't spoken to her yet. I still have a little time, but if they see her it's over. My thumbprints are on her throat like a signature.

Lucas narrows his eyes and looks at me. "You're acting so weird."

Everything is spinning—just as if I had actually been taking pills.

"We're about to go to the restaurant," says Kate. "Dad's booked a table for us at six. Are you guys going to get changed?"

Food? How am I supposed to eat? I can't exactly tell them about the letter when we're in the restaurant, can I?

Lucas points at his bright-green T-shirt. "What's wrong with this?"

"What do you think?"

"What about the yellow one, then? The one with the palm trees and the letters on it?"

Kate sighs. "Fender, can Lucas borrow a shirt?"

I take a deep breath. "I want . . ."

"Don't be awkward." Kate sighs. "It's just for one night. I'm going to go see if Linnea is in our room. See you soon!"

Before I can say anything else, she's headed down the hallway. I turn to look at Lucas, who is pulling one of my shirts out of my backpack. He squeezes his muscular arms into the sleeves and looks at me expectantly.

"How does it look?"

At that moment, there's an ear-piercing scream from the hallway, which penetrates every fiber of my body.

Kate.

Lucas and I hurry out and see Kate standing frozen in the doorway of her room. She's staring, wide-eyed, at something in front of her.

Linnea—that's the first thought that goes through my mind. Has something happened to her? Is it because of what I did?

But then I see what's going on. In the girls' room, someone has written words in big letters all over the walls. Even the windows are covered in black marker.

The room is one giant suicide note.

Slowly, we enter the room, one by one.

The words I so wanted to keep hidden from Kate are now grinning at her, in giant size.

This isn't right. I still had time left.

"*It's always dark for me*'?" Lucas reads out loud. "What *is* this?"

A different part of the letter is written on every wall. They're pieces of a puzzle that combine to form a horrifying image, an image I have two copies of inside my pocket.

"Fender. Lucas." Kate's voice sounds far away. "Look at this. . . ."

I follow her gaze to the wall behind the four-poster bed. Those letters seem to be extra big.

KATE, FENDER, AND LUCAS.
MY SO-CALLED BEST FRIENDS.

"What?" Lucas looks back at us. "How can . . . It's from . . ."

It's like he's run out of words.

"It's from Isolde." Kate looks at me with wide eyes. I wish I could act surprised, but I can't.

"This is my suicide note." Lucas's eyes dart to me. "This isn't real, is it? She can't have . . ."

For a year now, I've wanted to stop time and rewind everything, but never as much as now.

I want to go back to Kate's last birthday, when the four of us were sitting around the campfire and I was playing the guitar.

I want to change what happened, write a different ending to that night, but it's impossible.

Kate runs to the bathroom and I hear the sound of vomiting. This is just the beginning. She only knows a small part of the story.

"Fender?" Kate calls from the bathroom.

When I enter the bathroom, I'm shocked by her gray face. She looks at me like I just kicked her when she was down.

"You *knew* about this?"

At first I can't make any sense of Kate's words, but then

I see the mirror above the sink. There's a message, written in the same black marker, in the neat handwriting that I've come to recognize.

> *You thought I'd give you time*
> *to show them the letter yourself.*
> *Stupid Fender,*
> *do you really think you can trust me?*

SUITE

I just hope she's thirsty.

LINNEA

What have I gotten myself into? I'm in a hotel room with a boy I've known for only a few minutes.

But it feels really comfortable, like I've known Claus for months.

There's something about him that calms me. As if, for a moment, Fender and the stalker don't exist.

"Want a drink?" Without waiting for an answer, Claus opens the minibar and pours two glasses of soda.

I look around. Room 311 is on our floor, but at the opposite end of the hallway. There's a closed suitcase under the bed, but that's all. The comforter is completely smooth and unwrinkled. Claus probably didn't jump up and down on the bed like Kate and I did.

Will we ever do anything like that together again? As soon as I tell her the truth about Fender, Kate's going to take his side. And if I don't say anything, I'll have to go on acting normal when he's around. I don't know if I can do that. Fender has backed me into a corner.

"Hey, you keep things nice and neat, don't you?"

"I like to have things organized." Claus passes me a glass and sits down across from me. "Okay, now tell me. Why do you want to go home, why are you crying, and why are you spending so much time away from your friends?"

"That's a lot of questions."

"After that, it's your turn to ask questions." Claus smiles. "Don't worry. You can say whatever you like. It's safe with me."

Claus is right. He only knows my friends from that drinks party at the law firm. He isn't part of the gang, who have known one another so much longer than I've known them.

And then I start talking. It's like opening a stuffed closet, as all the words come tumbling out over each other.

"Kate and Lucas have always been nice to me. I feel comfortable with them. But it's different with Fender. There's something in his eyes that frightens me. Something dark. He sometimes stares at me so intensely that it's like he can see right through me. But then he'll just look past me, like I don't exist. Or it's the opposite, and he gets really aggressive toward me. Whenever I say something in class, he always has to disagree. It's wearing me out. Normally I'm good at standing up for myself, but not with Fender. He scares me."

"*Scares* you?"

"Don't laugh!"

Claus looks serious. "I'm not laughing. I just think it's . . . strange. He should be a friend of yours, not an enemy."

81

I nod. "It's because of Kate. He's her best friend, and she's my best friend. So we're stuck with each other."

"Sounds complicated."

"It is."

"But why does he scare you?"

"Well, he just tried to strangle me."

Claus's eyes widen behind his glasses. "What?"

I suddenly understand how crazy this must sound, so I sweep my braid, now dry, over my shoulder and lift my chin. "Here."

"I can see the bruises." Claus curses quietly. "That's not right. You need to make it clear to him that he has to stop."

"But that's the whole problem. I'm too scared."

"Why did he get so mad?"

"I asked him the wrong question."

I don't mention Isolde. Claus might feel guilty because he was the one who sent me in that direction.

"So now you want to go home because of this . . . Fender?"

"Not just because of him," I admit. "I'm being stalked." Now that I'm saying it out loud for the first time I can hear how unlikely it sounds. "It might sound crazy, but . . ."

"Not at all." Claus takes a swig from his glass. "Why do you think it sounds crazy?"

"Well, no one has any reason to stalk me. I don't have a disturbed ex, I'm not a celebrity, I'm . . ."

"Pretty."

Suddenly I don't know where to look.

"I didn't mean that in a creepy way," says Claus. "But if you ask me, a lot of guys would think you're pretty."

I think about Lucas, who flirts with me all the time. Could he be one of those guys?

"Maybe," I say quietly.

"And the fact that you're so modest makes you even more attractive, of course."

I turn the glass around in my hands.

"And what's the story with you?" I say, changing the subject.

Claus looks up. "What do you mean?"

"Like, do you have someone?"

There's a long silence. The only sound is the quiet buzzing of the minibar.

When Claus starts talking, his voice sounds different. Soft and cautious.

"A while ago, I was really, really in love."

I notice that he's talking in the past tense. It feels as if there is suddenly a huge distance between us, much bigger than the few feet between the chairs we're sitting in.

"You shouldn't go home. You need to stay here." Claus looks at me. "If you go home, this stalker's sure to follow you. And Fender will be back in your classroom as usual on Monday."

"So what should I do?"

"Confront Fender. Tell him what you think of him."

"Do you think that'll work?"

"You'll feel better if you get it out. Will you give it a try?"

"Yes." Hesitantly, I stand up. I'm not going to say anything to Kate and Lucas for now. I want to talk to Fender first.

"Are you leaving already?" asks Claus. He sounds disappointed.

"Yes, but thanks for the chat."

"Wait a minute." Claus comes and stands between me and the door. For a moment I think he wants to say something, but then he holds out my glass. "You didn't have your drink."

I look at the glass, but I still need to pee.

"No, I'm good, thanks," I say. "You have it."

The perfect opportunity: gone!
I throw the glass at the wall.
Shards of glass fly everywhere.
The soda, mixed with the sedative, fizzes on the carpet.

FENDER

"I've got to get this off." Kate is scrubbing at the wall over the bed with her sleeve.

"Kate . . . ," I say. "There's no point."

"You knew!" she suddenly screams. "You knew she was dead and you didn't tell us!"

The words hit me like bullets. Kate's right. I know that. I should have told her yesterday, right after the harbor.

"It's not true, is it?" Kate looks at me, pleading. "Tell me she's not dead."

I can see she's going through the same roller coaster of emotions as me. From fury to grief to denial and back again.

"I'm sorry," I say quietly.

Kate collapses, wrapping her hands over her head like a helmet. She rocks gently back and forth to the rhythm of her sobs.

I want to put my arm around her. I want to say that it's all one big nightmare.

"How long have you known?"

I jump at the sound of Lucas's voice.

"Since yesterday. I got a letter."

"You've known for a *day?*" Lucas looks at me in disbelief. "Do you have the letter here?"

I take the note and the copy of it from my pocket and give one to Lucas and the other to Kate.

While they're both reading, I gaze around the room. The words seem to come off the walls toward me, closing me in.

"Who gave you these letters?" Lucas looks at me. "Was it her?"

I shake my head. "Room service came to the door when you were at the pool. That was the silver dome that you saw in our room. Someone in the hotel is doing this."

The words struggle to come out, like syrup from a bottle.

"I found the first one on my doormat yesterday. He must have sent that one too."

"He?" echoes Lucas.

"Someone who knew her." I take the death notice from my jeans pocket. "He says we murdered her."

The color drains from Lucas's face. Cursing, he turns around and clutches his hair.

Kate looks at me through a haze of tears. Her mascara has left lines down her cheeks.

"You should have told us!" Kate gets to her feet. Standing on the mattress, she's more than a head taller than me.

Then she punches me in the chest.

"She was my best friend. And now she's dead."

I don't want her to say that. I don't want to hear it.

"Stop it."

"Why?" Kate hits me again. "It's true, isn't it? She's dead because of us! Because of what happened last year!"

Inside my head I hear the scream again. It's always there, like background music.

"Stop," I say. "Please."

"She's killed herself, Fender. She's dead. Dead. Dead. And soon everyone's going to find out. What do you think my dad will do when he sees this room? I might as well announce the news to everyone right now." Kate cups her hands around her mouth and starts shouting. "We're the ones who killed Is—"

"No!" With a shout, I push Kate down onto the bed and clamp my hand over her mouth. Within two seconds, I am sitting on top of her, pushing her arms down into the mattress with my knees.

"You need to shut your mouth," I growl.

The fury in Kate's eyes gives way to astonishment. The way she's looking at me . . .

That's how *she* looked too.

That night.

Staring up at the stars above.

There was blood. Blood everywhere.

Sticking to my hands, my face, my hair.

In the shower that night, the water turned pink.

It trickled between my toes and down the drain. I was literally washing her away.

"Fender!"

Lucas's voice brings me back to my senses. Beneath me, I see Kate staring at me with wide eyes.

"Get a grip, you idiot!" Lucas shoves me off Kate. I fall off the bed and hit my head on the wall.

I watch Lucas put his arm around Kate and help her up. She's not screaming now, just crying, without making any sound.

Her black hair is messed up, and there's a cut on her cheek where I scratched her.

"You can't do this," Lucas says, glaring at me. "I get that you're not yourself, but we're all in shock!"

First I attacked Linnea, and now Kate. What am I doing?

"Who delivered the room service?" asks Lucas.

I rub the back of my head. "I don't know. I think it was a man. I only heard his voice."

But was it a man? The voice was so muffled that it could just as easily have been a woman. And I certainly can't guess how old they were.

"You don't know?"

I shake my head.

"Linnea . . ."

Lucas and I both look up at the same time.

Kate's eyes are huge. "Linnea doesn't know about any of this."

Lucas curses. "We're not going to involve her. She has nothing to do with this."

"How do you intend to keep this hidden?" I say, pointing

89

at the walls. The words seem to be turning blacker and blacker.

"We have to clean it," says Lucas. "We need a bucket of soapy water and a bunch of scouring pads. The housekeepers here have all the stuff we'll need."

"It'll be one big disaster area . . ."

"Do you have a better idea?" Lucas snarls at me.

I shake my head. He's right. We have to try *something*.

"We'll keep Linnea away from here for now." I know how impossible that sounds. This is her room. She could be here any minute.

"Will you go find the cleaning stuff?" Lucas says. "I'll stay with Kate."

Normally it would be the other way around, but that was before I turned into a monster.

Kate still hasn't looked at me. She's sitting on the corner of the bed, as far away from me as possible.

I should say I'm sorry, but the words get stuck in my throat.

I struggle to my feet and walk to the door.

"Fender?"

I look back. Lucas has a strange look in his eyes. I've only seen that expression on his face once before, in the hospital a year ago. Kate and I were hugging, and over her shoulder I saw Lucas looking at me in exactly that same way.

"Yes?"

He pauses.

"Be careful."

"Okay." I look back at Kate, who is rocking slowly back and forth again. Can I ever put this right?

My legs shaking, I step out into the hallway and close the door behind me.

How am I supposed to persuade a housekeeper to lend me her things?

Maybe I should just go to the nearest supermarket. But where is it?

"Fender?"

Startled by the sound of my name, I turn around.

There, standing in front of me, is Linnea.

LINNEA

"Linnea." Fender gives me a strange look. "Hey."

A few strands of hair are sticking out of his bun and his shirt is crooked.

As always, there's an awkward silence between us, but this one lasts even longer than usual.

"Is Kate in there?" I ask finally.

"No." Fender blocks the way. "No, she's not."

His eyes are darting nervously back and forth. What's going on? Is he scared I'll tell Kate and Lucas what happened outside?

"I want to go past," I say.

"You can't."

"Why not?"

"We need to talk," says Fender. "About what just happened."

I shake my head. "No need."

"Please." I've never heard Fender say that word before, certainly not to me. "Come with me."

Fender leads the way to their room and holds the door open. "Just for a minute."

I hesitate. What if he attacks me again?

But then I remember what Claus said. I can run away from Fender, but on Monday I'll be back in the classroom with him.

"Fine," I say. "But yeah, just for a minute."

I walk into the room and sit down in an easy chair. Fender lingers at the door.

"I . . . I want to apologize. For . . ."

"For trying to strangle me," I say, finishing his sentence for him.

Fender blushes a little. That's a first too.

"Yes," he says then. "Yes, that."

There's another silence.

Where are Kate and Lucas? Still in the bar? I'm starting to get impatient.

"Was there anything else?"

Fender hooks his fingers together. "No, no, nothing."

"Good. Then there's something I'd like to say."

"Oh."

"You are such a jerk." The words come out less forcefully than I intended, but their effect is strong enough.

Fender's mouth falls open and he stares at me in disbelief. A muscle beside his eye is twitching.

"It's bad enough that you attack me with words every day, but if you ever put your hands on me again . . ."

I'm shaking, but now I can't stop.

"You went too far, and I'm not going to stand for it. You can't treat people like that."

Fender nods slowly but still doesn't say a word.

He's actually not that scary at all. Why didn't I see that before?

"Okay. Then I'd like to leave now." I stand up.

Fender stands between me and the door.

"I want to go to my room."

"You can't." Fender holds out his arms to block the way.

"It's *my* room!"

"Just stay here for a while."

What is going on? I try to get around Fender, but he just moves with me.

"Let me past," I say.

"No."

My heart is pounding faster and faster. I can feel my whole body heating up.

No, please, not now . . .

I glance back, but there's only a window. The only way out is this one.

"Get out of the way."

My hands are sweating, my head is tingling, my lungs are wheezing. Everything in my body is changing so quickly that I can't keep up with it.

I push against Fender's chest, but he's like a block of concrete.

"I . . ."

"Linnea?" I hear him say, but my name falls, along with me, into a black hole.

FENDER

Linnea collapses. I grab hold of her upper arms, but too late. She collapses to the floor, with her right leg bent under her.

"Linnea?!"

I rest my index and middle fingers on her neck and feel her heartbeat. She's still breathing.

Did she faint? But why?

I look around. She can't stay on the floor like that. I have to move her to the bed.

Linnea feels as heavy as lead, as if her whole body is working against me. With all my strength, I heave her up. As I lay her on the bed, her head flops onto my pillow. Her blond braid lies to one side.

She looks like her.

I don't want to see the resemblance, but it's there.

They have the same full lips, the same color hair, and the same freckles around their noses. Why did I never notice that before?

Linnea groans quietly.

I hurry to the bathroom and, as I'm coming back with a

95

glass of water, Linnea's eyes flutter open. They roll back in her head twice, but then focus on me.

"Fender?"

I take a step back.

"I . . . I didn't do anything," I say quickly. "You just collapsed."

Linnea mumbles something.

"Do you want some water?" I say, handing her the glass. "Can you sit up?"

Linnea pushes herself up from the mattress and drinks a few sips. "Could you . . . Could you fetch Kate?"

Kate?

I'm about to say yes, but then I remember that she's next door.

In a room full of writing.

With mascara running down her face.

"She's still in the bar," I lie. "We can go there in a minute. I just need to . . ."

"You're not leaving me here alone." Linnea grabs my wrist.

I sit back down on the bed. "Okay."

Linnea drinks the rest of the water and then puts the empty glass on the nightstand. Unsteadily, she sits up and swings her legs over the edge of the bed.

"What are you doing?"

"I really need to . . ." Linnea nods at the bathroom door.

"Oh, right," I say. "Can you manage on your own?"

Linnea raises her eyebrows.

"Go on," I say quickly. When Linnea locks the door, I give a deep sigh. Kate and Lucas are waiting next door. They're probably wondering where I am.

The toilet flushes and Linnea comes back into the room. More color is slowly appearing on her cheeks.

"Did I give you a fright?" she asks quietly.

"A bit," I admit. "Do you often faint?"

Linnea nods. "Sometimes. It usually happens when I feel trapped."

I blocked her way.

Now I understand. "So that's why you steer clear of elevators."

Linnea nods. "I hate them."

"Why?"

"I just do."

"No one hates something for no reason," I say.

"Except you hating me, right?"

She says it casually, as if it's nothing. I pretend not to hear her and take her glass back to the bathroom.

"When I was ten, I was allowed to go visit my grandpa and grandma on my own for the first time," I suddenly hear Linnea say. I stay in the bathroom, as I'm scared she'll stop telling her story otherwise.

"I took the elevator, because they lived on the sixth floor. I thought it would be much quicker than the stairs. But then it got stuck. I was in there for an hour and a half."

My breath catches in my throat. An hour and a half?!

"That's why I'll never use an elevator again."

"I get it," I say. My voice echoes off the tiles.

"What about you?" asks Linnea. "Is there anything you'll never do again?"

"Me? I'll never love anyone again," I blurt out.

Why did I say that? No one knows that. I didn't even know it myself until now.

I'm about to yell that it was just a joke, but at that moment there are three knocks on the door.

"Room service!"

LINNEA

Fender runs out of the bathroom. "Stay there!"

I look at him in surprise. "Why? Did you order something?"

"Just do as I say."

"Why are you whispering?"

Fender puts his hand on my shoulder and pushes me back onto the bed. He looks wired, like he might attack me again at any minute.

Fender walks to the door and looks through the peephole. Why is he acting so over the top? Anyone would think a serial murderer had just knocked on the door.

Fender swings the door open. He stands in the doorway for a few seconds and then stoops to pick something up. I hear the rustle of paper.

Then he quickly shuts the door and comes back to me.

"What was it?" I ask.

"Nothing."

He's lying. I thought he was finally being honest with me. The way he just answered my question about what he'd never do again, it came straight from the heart. Even though

I couldn't see his face when he said it, I could feel the pain in his reply.

"Would you empty your pockets?"

Fender looks like he's been stung by a wasp. "Why?"

"What did room service bring?"

"Nothing. It was a mistake."

"So it's something to do with that Isolde, right?"

And again Fender immediately reacts to the name. His face flushes red and he clenches his jaw. I can see that he's trying to come up with an answer, but no matter what he says, I doubt I'll believe him.

"I'm going to see Kate."

"No, you're not."

"Kate's *my* best friend too," I say. "And I'll do what I like. Maybe she can tell me who Isolde is."

"Leave her alone." Again, I see the Fender I saw outside the hotel.

It's like Fender is made up of lots of different Fenders. And each one is completely different.

"Why? What could be so bad?" I get up off the bed. "Is Isolde dead or something?"

I blurt out the words, but then I see Fender's reaction. His face is like a candle slowly flickering out.

So Isolde *is* dead.

Kate and Lucas must know about it, and they've kept it a secret from me. But why? What's so bad that they can't tell me?

"She was one of us." Fender suddenly starts talking. "She was my girlfriend and Kate's best friend. The four of us were always together."

So Isolde *was* part of their gang. Claus was right.

"How . . ." I weigh my words carefully. "How did it happen?"

"Suicide."

My heart thumps painfully against my ribs. Fender stares out the window, as if he can see something particularly interesting out there.

"Suicide?" I echo.

"Yes." Fender clutches the windowsill. "It happened this week. But she's actually been dead for 364 days."

For a moment, I think Fender must have been keeping count, but then I realize.

"So it was on Kate's birthday last year . . ."

"Something went very wrong."

I wanted to know the truth, but now that it's coming closer and closer, I feel more like running away.

"There's someone in the hotel who wants to punish us for last year."

I look at him. "What do you mean?"

"That room service just now. Someone's threatening us, sending us messages." Fender sighs. "We weren't going to tell you."

I was right. All three of them have been keeping it from me. I obviously knew they'd been friends for ages before I came along, but I had no idea there was something so huge going on.

"Tell me everything," I say.

Fender looks at me. "Are you sure?"

No.

"Yes," I say. "Certain."

Fender gives a deep sigh as he takes a gold envelope out of his pocket.

"This was just delivered by someone who calls himself Room Service. We don't know his real name, only that he's here in the hotel. He's been sending us messages, like her suicide note and the death notice from the newspaper. This message was under the cloche just now."

"The what?"

"Cloche. Like that one over there." Fender points at the silver dome in the corner of the room.

It was there when we came back from the pool.

We found Fender surrounded by chaos.

Had this already started then?

I point at the gold envelope in Fender's hand. "What's in there?"

"I haven't opened it yet." Fender looks at me. "But there's something else you need to know."

"What's that?"

"Before, it just had the names of Lucas, Kate, and me on it, but . . ." Fender turns the envelope to show me. "Now yours is there too."

I stare at the six letters in front of me.

"How . . ." I stammer. "How does he know my name?"

"He knows everything." Fender puts the envelope back into his pocket.

"I'm going to the bar." I walk to the door. I want to hear the whole story from Kate. I need to know what happened last year.

"They're not in the bar." Fender blushes a little. "They're next door."

"In our room?"

So that's why I wasn't allowed in there. Were they having a meeting to discuss how to keep me out of everything?

I feel tears prickling my eyes. Am I worth nothing at all to them?

I thought Kate and I were friends! I felt like Lucas and I were getting closer lately, but clearly not close enough for him to tell me the truth.

"Come on." Fender holds the door open for me. "Now that you know, I'll show you."

We go out into the hallway. Fender knocks on our door twice.

"Fender?" comes a voice.

"Yeah."

The door swings open, and Lucas is standing there. He pauses when he sees me, but then he lays into Fender.

"What are you doing? We were going to keep her out of this!"

I can feel myself getting smaller and smaller. Lucas is talking about me as if I'm not here. Why are they doing this? What could be so bad that they don't dare trust me?

But then I see the room.

Our beautiful room.

There's nothing left of it.

It reminds me of the bridge downtown, completely covered in graffiti.

Individual words, scraps of sentences, and my friends' names are written all over the room. I stare at the words above the bed.

KATE, FENDER, AND LUCAS.
MY SO-CALLED BEST FRIENDS.

"It's from the suicide note." Fender is standing behind me. "Room Service left this here for us."

"What are you doing?" cries Lucas.

"She already knows," hisses Fender. "So what difference does it make?"

I read all the words and try to solve the puzzle, but at the same time I'm not sure I really want to.

My name isn't on the wall, but it *is* on the envelope. Why does Room Service think I have something to do with this? I wasn't even around last year on Kate's birthday! He has the wrong person.

I turn on my heels.

"What are you doing?" asks Fender.

"Going home," I say. "This is your past, not mine."

I should have left straightaway, before I went with Claus to his room. I don't want anything to do with this. This is some really sick stuff.

"Good," Fender says. "You go."

"Wh-what?" Lucas stammers in surprise.

"She's right." Fender looks at him. "She has nothing to do with this. If she wants to go, she can go."

I look at Kate. Her eyes are so puffy. It looks like she's cried gallons of tears.

Why did she never tell me anything about Isolde?

She was her best friend!

And what happened last year that made Room Service want to punish them?

I remember what Lucas said in the bar.

Kate thinks we're all best friends forever.

Are there other things I don't know? It's like this is just the tip of the iceberg, and the rest is still underwater.

I look at the words above the bed again.

My so-called best friends.

Did they betray Isolde? But how? Did she feel as lonely within the gang as I do? Maybe she was an outsider too.

I look at Kate again. She's staring at her sneakers. Who are my "friends" really? How can they call themselves friends if they can lie to me like that? An hour ago, Lucas even claimed not to know Isolde at all!

The hallway is calling to me. *Leave. This is your chance! Go!*

But if I go now, I'll never get answers to the questions I haven't even asked yet.

"He has us in a corner, but he doesn't have anything to attack you with," says Fender. He is still holding the door open.

Yes, he does, I want to say, but I swallow my words.

"Close it." I cross my arms. "I'm staying."

Something tells me this is the most stupid choice I could make, but I need answers. I have to know what the three of them have been hiding from me all this time. And if anything about the past nine months was real.

"Are you sure?" Am I just imagining it or was there a hint of respect in Fender's voice?

"Absolutely certain."

"Okay." Fender closes the door. "In that case: welcome aboard."

FENDER

She's staying.

"Linnea, I . . ." Kate starts to say something, but Linnea cuts her off.

"I want to know what's inside that envelope."

It's like she's standing straighter and straighter. There's nothing left of the Linnea I know, who was always hiding in the background.

"What envelope?" asks Kate.

I hold it up. It's like throwing a hand grenade into the room. Her eyes grow wide with panic.

"Another delivery from Room Service?"

I nod and open the envelope. All my muscles tense as I take out the paper.

They're torn-out pages with a cartoonish picture of a mouse on them. The paper looks vaguely familiar.

I feel a stabbing pain in my chest, as if something is trying to claw its way out from inside.

Suddenly I remember where I've seen this paper before.

It's from her diary.

Happy birthday to Kate.

Tomorrow.

I don't want to go.

I want to pull the covers over my head and pretend
*   I'm sick.*

But she's my best friend and the boys will be there too.

I can't cancel.

They'll ask questions I can't answer.

I'm so scared about how all of this is going to end.

She sometimes used to write in her diary when I was there. I'd lie in bed and she'd sit in the window seat.

It was one of those kids' diaries, with a little padlock on it, which are so easy to open. But . . . why would I have done that? We didn't have any big secrets from each other. She used to tell me the things that mattered.

Or so I thought.

"What is this?" Lucas is looking over my shoulder.

I stare at the letters, which are dancing on the paper. They swirl around, doing pirouettes.

"Th—this is impossible . . . ," I stammer.

"Did she *really* write this?" Kate comes and stands with me too.

I nod, but it feels like my head is falling. I point at the mouse.

"I recognize that."

"What was Isolde talking about?" Kate looks at me. "Why was she dreading my birthday?"

"I don't know."

Did she have some kind of premonition? Did she know that day would end so badly?

Why did she never confide in me? It's like I'm reading about a completely different life, the life of another girl entirely.

"It's fake." Kate snatches the paper from my hand. "Room Service has faked her diary."

I stare at the letters, handwriting that very few people could read. Her writing was like her bedroom: chaotic. Whenever her mom and dad let her work with them in the hair salon, she left scissors and clips all over the place.

"How did that madman get hold of her diary?" Linnea's question hangs in the air.

No one knows, but I can see that everyone's searching for the answer.

"Maybe she gave it to him." Kate glances my way. I know what she's thinking, because it's a thought that already shot through my head too. It has to be someone she knew, someone she trusted.

A new boyfriend.

So it's true?

"There's more," says Kate. "Want me to read it out loud?"

"No." Lucas shakes his head furiously. "I've heard enough.

Please, just leave the rest. He has her diary. Fine. But how does that help us?"

He's kind of right. What's the point of reading more?

But this is *her* diary, *her* feelings.

The truth, no matter how much it's going to hurt.

These are the things she never dared say to me.

The only thing I can do is read on.

This afternoon he was here.
Of course he was.
He watched me from a distance.
He thought I couldn't see.
But I always see him.
I want to tell Fender everything.
But then I'll have to be one hundred percent honest
*   with him.*
I don't know if I dare.

Kate reads out the last sentence, because my voice is trembling too much. I put down the paper and clench my jaw.

"Fender . . . ?"

I don't want to look up. I don't want to see Kate's pity. Something is bubbling up inside me and it wants to come out.

What was she up to?

Who is this about?

A he.

A boy.

Someone else.

No, it's impossible.

I think about all our moments together at the harbor, under our little boat.

We sometimes sat there together for hours, talking and kissing. If something had been wrong, I'd have noticed, wouldn't I?

"I'm not going to listen to this anymore." Lucas crosses his arms. "Someone's trying to drive you crazy, Fender. You need to realize that!"

But I still read on.

Tonight he was across the street.
He must have been waiting for Fender to leave.
I went outside. Think I gave him a fright.
"This has to stop," I say.
"What do you mean?"
"What do you want from me?"
"Hey, you know what I want."
He tried to kiss me, but this time I turned
*   my face away.*

I crush the paper. The picture of the mouse crumples in my hand.

"Fender . . . ," Kate pleads. "Just stop."
But there's one bit left.

I have to be honest with Fender.
But how do I do that?
Maybe I should just start by writing his name here:
Claus.

LINNEA

"Who's Claus?" asks Kate quietly.

The name buzzes through every cell in my body.

The boy who called me a candy-machine whisperer. The boy who listened to me and gave me advice about Fender. Less than an hour ago, I was in his room.

He is Room Service.

"He's about our age, with black hair and glasses."

All eyes are on me now.

"What?" Kate stammers. "How do you know that?"

"Because I know someone called Claus." I feel myself becoming dizzy again, like I could faint at any minute. "And he's here. At the Riverside."

"You have to tell us everything." Kate sits me down on one of the easy chairs and crouches down in front of me. Fender is in the other chair. Lucas is standing by the window.

"So how do you know him?"

"I only met him this afternoon. He's staying here. You guys know him too."

"What?" Kate frowns. "I don't know anyone called Claus."

"Yes, you do. You guys met him once at a drinks party at Kate's dad's firm. That's where he knew Isolde from too."

Kate shakes her head. "Wait a moment. I don't get it. How did this Claus end up at my dad's drinks party?"

"His parents work for him."

Kate looks at me. "There aren't any couples working for Dad. It's all young men and women, without children. My dad's the only one with a family."

So Claus was lying.

Then who was that couple in the hallway?

I thought Claus looked like the woman, but how well could I see her from that distance? Of course I believed they were his parents. Why would he lie about something like that?

"Who is Claus?" Kate asks Fender again.

"Someone she used to know. She said he didn't matter."

Fender's face is white as a sheet. It's bad enough that Claus lied to me, but Fender is just finding out that his girl-friend was leading a double life. So clearly that Claus guy did matter. The way Isolde writes about him is pretty intense.

Absentmindedly, Kate slips the gold envelope through her hands. She doesn't say anything. No one says anything. But then suddenly she looks up in surprise.

"Guys, there's something else in here."

Kate takes a last sheet of paper out of the envelope. It's a lot smaller, with just a few sentences on it. As her eyes run over the words, all the color leaves her face.

"What is it?" I ask.

Kate looks at me. "It's the rules of the game," she says.

RULES OF THE GAME

IF YOU WANT ANSWERS

1. *Stay in the hotel.*
2. *Don't call in any help.*
3. *When Room Service knocks, wait for a minute before opening the door.*
4. *Act as normal as possible.*
5. *Don't go looking for me.*

LOBBY

FENDER

Claus.

She once mentioned him in passing.

They went on a few dates, but he liked her more than she liked him.

They lost touch.

I thought.

She said he didn't matter.

So how did he get her diary?

"Rules of the game?" Lucas spits out the words. "Has he gone totally insane? You're not going to listen to this, are you?"

"Calm down," says Kate.

"Calm down?" Lucas shrieks. "Why would I do that?"

"Because . . ." Kate pauses. "For Fender."

I look up. Everyone is staring at me. Even Linnea.

Stupid Fender, who was being cheated on and didn't realize.

Stupid Fender, who thought he was the only guy for her.

Stupid Fender, who thought the worst thing that could happen to him was reading her letter.

"I . . . I'm just going to my room for a while."

"I'll go with you." Lucas is already heading off into the hallway, but I shake my head.

"I want to be alone for a bit."

Lucas exchanges a quick look with Kate.

"Honestly," I add. "I'll see you later."

Without waiting for an answer, I escape into the hallway.

Our room is still intact, but it feels as wrecked as the girls' room. I can't see the luxury anymore. It's like a thick layer of dust is lying over it.

I place the diary page in front of me on the bed and stare at the words.

This time I turned my face away.

That sentence keeps repeating itself inside my head.

What did she mean by *this time*?

They saw each other the night before Kate's party, exactly a year ago now.

What happened then?

Why is Claus sending us these messages?

Maybe Lucas is right and Claus is trying to drive me crazy.

Because I had something he would never have: *her.*

I frantically think back to the night before Kate's birthday. I was so enthusiastic about her plans for the weekend. We were going to camp in the woods just outside town. Kate had arranged for two double tents and a big supply of food and drink.

I couldn't wait to be lying inside the same tent as her, close together.

Should I have noticed then that something was wrong?

Was I so blinded by my feelings for her that I didn't realize she was worried about something?

Could I have seen Claus when I cycled away? He was probably already standing in the bushes, waiting for me to leave.

I drive my nails into my palms. I want to find that boy and thump him in the face. I want to hurt Claus as much with my fists as he's hurt me with his messages.

I want . . .

Yes, what do I want?

I want my memories of her to remain as they were.

There are times when hearing *nothing* is better than hearing *something*.

I get up off the bed and walk to the window. A golden glow is shining over the houses.

Normally I'd think this view was amazing. Even romantic. Now all I want to do is open the windows and jump out. Disappear into the dark river and never surface.

Is that how she felt this week?

Is that why she did it?

I open the window and the fresh evening breeze hits my face.

Why didn't she say something to me?

How many times did they kiss without me knowing?

Tongues wrapped around each other.

His hands in *her* hair.

The hair I'd run my hands through too.

Why didn't I notice anything?

Down below, a tour boat goes past, with cheerful music playing.

I look down. It seems much higher than four stories.

Suddenly I picture her earlier this week, standing on a tall building. Maybe she jumped. Is that how she killed herself?

Am I brave enough to do the same?

I put one foot on the windowsill and pull myself up. Crouching there, I look down and judge the distance.

What was she thinking about before she did it? About me or about him?

"Don't do it," a voice says behind me. "Please."

LINNEA

"Don't do it. Please."

Fender is crouched on the windowsill. When he turns around, he looks at me with haunted eyes.

For a moment, he doesn't seem to recognize me, but then he says: "I thought I told you I wanted to be alone."

"So you could commit suicide too?"

My breath is racing. I could tell something was going on. A little voice inside me told me I had to go to Fender. I was halfway down the stairs to meet Kate and Lucas in the bar when I turned around. They're waiting in the bar now, with no idea what's going on.

"I'm not committing suicide." But Fender stays there in the window.

"You're going to fall."

"What do you care?"

I ignore his comment.

"I don't know what exactly was going on between Isolde and Claus, but I think it was mainly him chasing after *her*."

"How would you know that?"

"Because I know what it's like to be stalked."

Fender's eyes narrow. I have to be honest with him, even though he might not believe me.

Linnea sees things that aren't there.

"When you found me in the park last night, I didn't just fall off my bike. Someone was following me, and I was trying to get away." I take a deep breath. "At the pool, I had the feeling I was being watched again, and I saw a shadow darting away. I thought I was losing my mind, but his bike is parked in front of the hotel. I think it's Claus. That means he was spying on Isolde first—and now me."

All kinds of noises are coming in from the street, but inside this room time is standing still.

Claus and my stalker are the same person. When Fender read out the pages from Isolde's diary, I understood. What Isolde described felt so very familiar.

"So that's why you were so afraid in the park?" Fender asks. "And it wasn't because of . . ."

"Because of you?" I shake my head. "No. Not that time."

Fender's eyes go to my throat. "Oh."

He looks back outside. I have to keep him talking, because then at least he won't jump.

"We need to stop this Claus guy. He's done enough damage already."

"Where do you want to start looking? This hotel is huge!"

"Room 311," I say.

Fender snorts. "Or Room 248. Or Room 194. Or all the rooms between, or above, or below."

I shake my head. "No. I'm certain. I've been inside his room."

Fender looks up in astonishment. And then everything happens at once.

Fender starts to wobble, and his foot slips.

I leap forward and grab him by his denim jacket. When I give it a firm tug, there's a ripping sound.

For a moment, I think Fender's going to tumble out of the window anyway, but then we fall back into the room together. I bang my arm on the coffee table, and Fender lands on my legs.

Heart pounding, breath wheezing, I lie there on the floor. Fender is panting like he just ran a marathon.

What would have happened if I hadn't grabbed him in time?

The minutes pass, but neither of us stands up. We both stare at the ceiling.

Finally Fender breaks the silence. "Why did you follow me?"

"I could feel something was up."

"You could *feel* it?"

"Yes, what's wrong with that?"

"Nothing," says Fender quickly. "Nothing."

My heartbeat slowly returns to normal.

"Thank you," Fender says.

"What for?"

"For not saying anything to Kate and Lucas about what happened outside."

"I just haven't gotten around to it yet."

Fender stands up and closes the window. He doesn't thank me for saving his life.

"You coming?"

"Where to?"

Fender opens the door. "To talk to Claus."

My heart rate shoots straight back up again. "But we can't. The rules of the game . . ."

"I don't care." Fender's eyes are shooting fire. "Are you coming or not?"

If I let Fender go alone, he'll be risking his life. What if he attacks Claus, like he attacked me? Claus could be armed. . . .

"Then I'll go on my own." Without saying anything else, Fender moves out into the hallway.

I sit on the floor for a few more seconds, but then scramble to my feet.

"Fender!" I shout. "Wait!"

I catch up with Fender. He's striding along the hallway, his face tense. His fury is almost palpable, like a third person between us.

"What are you going to do?" I ask.

"Just talk to him."

I need to stop him, yet I know I won't be able to. Of course not. Claus has destroyed him.

"Here it is." Fender stops in front of Room 311. I look at the gold numbers on the door.

126

I try to imagine how Claus is going to react when he opens the door.

Will I get to see a completely different Claus?

The one I got to know was anything but scary.

But he was the one who put me on Isolde's trail. Did he actually want me to mention her to Fender?

Was I the spark that was supposed to make everything explode?

Was I Claus's pawn?

I'm startled by three loud bangs, as Fender slams his fist into the door. He looks as if he'd like to punch his way straight through it.

When there's no reaction from inside, Fender bangs three more times.

Again there's no answer.

"He's not there," I say quietly. "Come on. Let's go back to the others."

But then the door swings open.

FENDER

All my anger flows into this one moment. Claus doesn't even get a chance to say anything because I grab his jacket and pull him out into the hallway.

He falls onto his knees and starts shouting, but his words don't get through to me. Even what Linnea says completely passes me by.

How did he dare go see her when I was there with her?

How did he dare destroy Kate again? He has no idea what kind of hell we've been through this past year.

I raise my fist and look into his eyes.

"Admit it," I say with a voice that sounds like it doesn't belong to me. "Admit that she didn't want you anymore!"

"Fender!" Linnea is hanging on my arm. "Fender, it's not him."

"Admit it, you filthy, disgusting—"

"Fender, listen. This isn't Claus!"

Slowly, Linnea's words get through to me. It's like I was looking through the wrong lenses, as the man suddenly comes into focus. He's way too old to be Claus. He has to be in his thirties. Besides, he's not wearing glasses, and his hair is brown, not black.

Shocked, I let go of him.

"Are you out of your mind?" The man scrambles to his feet and shoves me hard into the doorpost. "What's the deal?"

"Sorry." Linnea quickly steps forward. "It was a misunderstanding."

"Say what?" The man furiously straightens his jacket. One of the buttons is missing. I can see it on the floor by my feet.

"First I find broken glass all over my room. Then I see that someone's been at my minibar. And now this!"

"Broken glass?" echoes Linnea, looking past the man and into the room.

"Yes, glass." The man's eyes are ablaze. "And what are you looking at?"

"Is this . . . your room?"

"Yes, of course this is my room! Are you two leaving now? I'm calling Security."

Linnea grabs me by the arm and pulls me down the hallway. We keep running until we get back to the stairs—and then she stops.

"Why didn't you listen?" she fires at me.

Nervously, I crack my fingers. I just attacked someone for the third time today. And it was the wrong person. I'm a ticking time bomb, and I keep going off.

"What am I supposed to do if you send me to the wrong room?" I say.

"That was the *right* room! I was just in there with Claus."

I shake my head. "Then how come that man . . ."

"Didn't you hear what he said? About finding a broken glass? And about someone using his minibar?"

"So?"

"Claus offered me a drink and tried to insist that I drink it before I left. When I didn't, he must have gotten so mad that he smashed it."

"Why would he get that mad at you for turning down a drink?"

As I say the words, it dawns on me. A wave of nausea washes over me, and I desperately try to swallow it away.

Would he really go so far as to put something in Linnea's drink?

What if Linnea had actually drunk it? None of us knew she was in his room.

Where is he now? That wasn't his room, so he could be anywhere. He can see us, but we can't see him.

I realize that Linnea is trying not to cry and I resist the urge to put my arm around her.

"Hey." Instead, I give her a nudge. "It's going to be okay. We're going to get him."

LINNEA

"You guys did *what?*" Lucas stares at us. "Have you completely lost it? 'Don't go looking for me.' How clear do the rules need to be?"

"Wouldn't you have done exactly the same?" I ask. "We had to give it a try."

"He didn't open the door?" Kate guesses.

"It wasn't his room." I feel nauseous again. "He took me to someone else's room."

I look around. It's just like Fender said. Claus could be anywhere. Even here in the bar, I don't feel safe.

I know how good Claus is at stalking. All that time, I had no idea it was him. It was me who approached him at the candy machine. I told him about my stalker. I confided in him.

He must have thought it was so amusing.

I thought it couldn't be Claus, because he seemed so friendly. How naive can you be? Even the most dangerous serial killers can turn on the charm.

"So how is Claus getting into these rooms?" asks Kate.

"I think he has a master key." Fender sighs. "That must be how he got into your room to write that letter all over the walls."

Kate shivers. "The thought of him being able to walk in and out whenever he wants . . ."

"Try not to think about it. Kate's dad made a dinner reservation for us. Let's go eat."

"Eat?" I stare at Lucas in astonishment. "You actually want to go have a nice meal out?"

"So what are we supposed to do?" Lucas says. "We were told to act as normal as possible. That's what it says in the rules. Anyway, we have to eat something, especially if this goes on all night."

I try not to think about the fact that Lucas could be right. Who knows when this is all going to end?

"He's right." Fender looks at Kate and me. "It's ridiculous, but we have to do it."

I know I won't be able to eat a bite.

I rub my arms. Is it really that cold in here, or is it the tension?

"I'm going to fetch my hoodie." I stand up. "See you in a minute."

"Kate will go with you."

I look at Fender in surprise. "Why?"

"You're not going alone."

Reluctantly, I go upstairs with Kate. As we walk up the

three flights of stairs, she doesn't say a word, but when we get to our room, she grabs my wrist.

"I'm sorry, Spinner. I know you're mad at me, but . . ."

I look at her. "I'm not mad."

"Disappointed, then?"

"I feel . . . betrayed."

Kate's face clouds over. "That was never the idea."

"Why did you never say anything about Isolde?"

"Where was I supposed to begin?" Kate runs her hand through her hair. "By saying that I had a best friend but that she left town last year to get as far away from us as possible?"

"That would have been a start."

I turn the key in the lock. As I enter the room, the feeling that I'm walking onto the set of a horror movie hits me again. The black letters grin at me from every wall.

I quickly unzip my weekend bag and take out my gray hoodie. I want to get out of here as soon as possible. Every minute in this room is one minute too many. I'm never going to be able to sleep in here.

"Do you need anything?" I ask.

But then I see Kate. She's staring with wide eyes at something behind me.

I turn to look. "What's wrong?"

"There." Kate points at the corner of the room. I was distracted by all the angry words, but then I see it.

"The bear," I stammer.

Lucas's gift, the huge teddy bear that was as big as Kate herself, has disappeared.

In its place, there's a note with a brief message.

One of you is the sacrifice.
You can decide for yourselves who comes to get the bear.
Come to the first balcony by the lobby at eight o'clock.
Come alone.

FENDER

I stare at the words. The sounds in the bar fade into the background.

"So this is what he wants," whispers Kate. I can see the panic in her eyes. "He wants us to sacrifice someone."

"Of course he doesn't," I say.

"That's what it says!"

"But we're not going to do that," I say quickly. "We'll think of something."

The dinner looks delicious, but we barely eat anything. Normally I'd really enjoy the meal, but I can't swallow a bite.

"We could tell your dad, Kate," I say. "He's a lawyer. He could help us."

"*Don't call in any help,*" says Kate. "Have you forgotten the rules? Anyway, my dad will lose it if he hears about this."

I fiddle with my napkin. "So what should we do?"

"We do what he says." Linnea hasn't said much so far, but now her words hit hard when she says: "I'll sacrifice myself."

"No!" Lucas and I both shout.

"It'd be suicide." Lucas blushes a deep red. "Sorry, Fender, I mean . . ."

I ignore him. "It's way too dangerous."

"It's the safest option," says Linnea. "And he won't do anything on the balcony, not with all those people there."

Lucas and I are about to object again, but Kate speaks first.

"All those people. That's it!"

"Not so loud!" I look around. What if Claus is listening in? We'd be better off discussing this upstairs.

"What exactly do you mean?"

Kate leans over the table. "We have to make Claus think that Linnea's coming alone."

"He'll see through it," says Lucas. "He outsmarts us every time."

"Not if we distract him with a crowd of people. His attention will slip—and we'll be one step ahead of him."

"And how are you going to manage that?"

"With a performance." Kate looks at me over her half-empty plate. "By you."

LINNEA

"No." Lucas shakes his head. "No, we are not going to do that."

"It'll work." Kate looks at me. "When Fender plays, lots of people are sure to come listen. Claus will be distracted and won't realize that one of us has come with you."

I nod slowly. Kate's right. Claus will think we're doing exactly as he's asking, but secretly someone will be with me.

"Who wants to be my backup?" I ask.

"We are not doing this." Lucas shoves back his chair. "We're not sacrificing anyone!"

He throws his napkin onto the table and storms off toward the doors to the courtyard. All three of us watch as he disappears outside.

"I'll go after him." I push back my chair too, squeeze between two tables, and follow him outside.

In spite of everything, the beauty of the Riverside still hits me.

The courtyard garden is huge and enclosed within the walls of the hotel. There are a few large trees out there, with strings of lights that give off a warm yellow glow.

In the middle of the courtyard is a fire pit, and pairs of diners are dotted around it.

I spot Lucas in a sheltered spot, close to the fire. When I go sit beside him, I can feel its heat. The wood is crackling and I hold out my hands to warm them.

"What's up?" I ask quietly.

"I don't want this to happen." Lucas looks at the flames. "I don't want you to sacrifice yourself. Whatever that means. I'm not leaving you alone with a dangerous lunatic."

"Someone has to do it."

Lucas sighs. "Not you."

"Why not?"

Suddenly, I feel two warm lips on mine. I'm so startled that I make a weird noise.

Lucas pulls me toward him, with one hand under my braid.

The whole back of my head tingles.

This is Lucas—that thought keeps shooting through my head. The boy I've known for nine months, who always flirts with me. And I thought it didn't mean anything.

Then he suddenly lets me go.

"Now you have your answer." Lucas gives me a cautious smile. "That's why you can't go."

If you ask me, a lot of guys would think you're pretty.

Claus's words flash through my mind. Had he already realized that Lucas likes me? How long has he been watching me?

I look around. The Riverside's windows are everywhere. The four floors wrap all around the garden.

Is Claus at one of those windows? Someone from the hotel comes to ask if we want a drink, and we both order cappuccinos.

As we sit slurping the foam, someone throws another log onto the fire.

For a moment, Claus fades into the background. It feels like we're just having a weekend away.

"What was she like?" I ask then. "Isolde?"

"Why do you want to know?" asks Lucas.

"Because I want to know who started all this."

"Why don't you ask Kate?"

"I'm asking you." I think back to the moment in the bar. "Or are you going to keep claiming not to know her?"

Lucas shakes his head. "She was . . . fierce. You didn't want to start a fight with her, because a completely different girl would emerge. But if she liked you, then she was sweet and caring. And she was great at thinking up gifts."

What if Kate's plan fails and Claus realizes I'm not coming alone?

"Isolde was chaotic. She was always losing her homework. Her mom and dad had a hair salon, here in town. She sometimes used to help out on Saturdays and she couldn't even remember if the customers wanted coffee or tea. And she couldn't make decisions either. She kept changing her mind about absolutely everything."

"And how was the friendship between her and Kate?"

"Isolde kept Kate's feet on the ground. She was never impressed whenever Kate's mom and dad gave her something new. She'd have thought this night at the Riverside was ridiculous—and she probably wouldn't have made a secret of it. That might have caused some friction."

I look into the flames. "It sounds . . . intense."

"It was. But it worked between the four of us. Kate was really good for Isolde too, because Isolde was a real worrier. Kate often used to change her mood by dragging her out with us."

"Why didn't anyone ever spill the beans? The whole school must have known her. Why didn't a student or a teacher mention her name even once?"

"It's off-limits." Lucas makes a face. "No one wants to talk about her because it's too painful."

I slowly nod. The fire crackles.

"I'll go with you," Lucas says then.

When I look up, he smiles.

"If we're really going ahead with this plan, I'll be the one who goes with you."

I feel a kind of warm glow inside. It already seems a bit less frightening now that Lucas will be there.

"Good."

Lucas looks at me. "Try not to imagine everything that could go wrong."

I give him a weak smile. "Well, they do call me Spinner for a reason."

"Spinner?"

"Yes, because I'm always imagining stuff. Something to do with spinning yarns. It's Kate's nickname for me. Lame, huh?"

Lucas flushes. "Sorry to tell you this, but Spinner was Isolde's nickname."

What is Lucas talking about? Why would Kate give me the same nickname as her old best friend?

Maybe because, all along, I've just been a replacement.

The idea echoes around inside my head and won't let me go.

What if Kate isn't the only one who sees the similarity with Isolde?

Perhaps that's why Fender has such a problem with me.

The fire suddenly feels hot and unpleasant.

"Where are you going?" Lucas asks when I stand up.

"We have to get back inside." I try to make my voice sound as normal as possible. "It's nearly eight."

FENDER

"We're back." Linnea's face is taut, as if someone has edited her in Photoshop. "Shall we go?"

Kate nods. "Is everything okay?"

"Fine," says Linnea, but her voice sounds strained. Did something happen outside?

"We're going to do it," says Lucas. "I'm going with Linnea."

"You?" I ask in surprise. Did they decide that outside?

"You're playing, Kate's watching, Linnea goes to the balcony, and I grab Claus." Lucas makes it sound so simple that I almost believe it.

"Are you sure?" asks Kate.

"Yes." Lucas looks at me. "And please play it like the musical genius you are."

—

The grand piano in the lobby gleams at me. I intertwine my fingers, which are shaking nonstop. What if I can't do it? Sure, I can get a tune out of a piano, but the guitar has always been my instrument.

"Does everyone know what to do?" Kate looks at all three of us.

It's quiet in the lobby. I really hope more people will come along soon.

What if Claus realizes what we're up to? What if he notices that Linnea isn't coming alone?

I look up at the first balcony out of the corner of my eye. There's no one there, and definitely not a boy with black hair and glasses.

"Yes, we do," says Lucas. "Don't we?"

Everyone nods. Linnea's face is still tense.

Is she scared? I want to tell her she doesn't have to sacrifice herself, but this is her own choice. She doesn't have to go along with Claus's plan, whatever it is.

"Then let's do it. And please be careful," Kate says to Linnea.

"I will." Linnea's voice sounds flat. "Hey, Spinner's got this."

Spinner?

"Fender, go." Kate gives me a gentle push. I can't ask what Linnea meant, because now it's time for me to give the performance of my life.

Everything depends on how well I do this. I have to make sure I get the attention of everyone in the entire hotel.

The grand piano seems twice as big as it did this afternoon. How am I supposed to play this thing?

The last time I played piano was in the music room at

school. She and I often used to go there when we wanted to be alone for a while.

She would always sit and watch me play. Sometimes she'd come and stand behind me halfway through the song and put her arms around me.

She'd playfully bite my earlobe until I had to stop because I couldn't concentrate.

I sit down on the stool, which creaks quietly under my weight.

I can see myself in the gleaming surface of the piano. Big, scared eyes.

The keys are so clean and white that it's like no one has ever played it before. I gently stroke them, my breath coming in starts.

If I don't calm down, I'm going to put Linnea in danger. Linnea, who has nothing to do with this, but who has stayed in the lion's den, for us.

I look up. Kate and Lucas look tense. Linnea is standing a few feet away from them.

Why aren't they acting normally? You can see from miles away that something is wrong.

I play the first notes. They boom so loudly around the room that I pull my hands away in shock.

It's as if the entire hotel is filled with my C chord.

The piano in the school music room is a joke compared to this thing. This piano is the real deal.

I look at my friends again. Kate gives me a forceful nod, so I have to go on playing.

I hit the C chord again, but this time I continue.

I play cautiously at first, but my fingers soon get used to the instrument. They become one with the keys, as if they've been friends for years.

A song begins to take shape under my fingers.

A song I played before.

For her.

I glance up. The balconies are empty, but I'm sure Claus is up there somewhere. He'll be waiting for Linnea to come to him. Our sacrifice.

An elderly couple pauses in the lobby, by the piano. They smile at me and nod approvingly. The receptionist even steps out from behind her desk.

It gives me the courage to keep playing.

A group of Japanese tourists stops too, and one of them takes a photograph.

A family with young children lingers at the entrance.

It's working!

I start singing. Without thinking about it, I sing the song for her. She used to love it. It was her favorite song of mine.

I sing as if my life depends on it. Or actually, Linnea's.

More people come to stand around the piano.

I sing as if she's standing behind me again, with her arms around me. Her warm breath on the back of my neck.

There are millions of musicians all over the world, but when I played, she looked at me as if I was the only one who could do this.

As if I was unique.

I play as if she's here. I have goose bumps on my arms when I start the chorus. The tempo goes up a bit, and my fingers find it tricky to keep up with the rhythm, but I get there.

I play as if she's lying under me on the bed. We used to spend hours just looking at each other and kissing.

When her dad called us for dinner, we often realized we'd missed lunch.

More people come and stand around me. The lobby is filling up and people are stopping to listen from the balconies too.

I see Kate standing in the audience. Linnea and Lucas have left.

Is this going to work?

Don't go looking for me.

At that moment, I miss the key and play a wrong note.

LINNEA

He is playing for her.

I feel it as soon as he begins. It's like a funeral speech, but a musical one.

He wasn't able to say goodbye to her, so he's doing it this way instead.

For a moment, I forget everything. I can only look at the boy in front of me.

"Linnea," hisses Kate. "Go."

I want to lash out at her, but I swallow the words. This is not the time. When all of this is over, I'm going to confront her about that nickname. Then I'll tell her that she's lost me. That I don't want to be a replacement for Isolde anymore. I want a friend who's honest, who wants me as I am. Not someone who's using me to fill a gap.

I look at Fender, who's still playing. It's as if he's somewhere else entirely again, but this time I don't find it scary at all.

For the first time, I understand what Isolde must have seen in him.

His bun is messy, the sleeves of his denim jacket and shirt are rolled up sloppily, but he looks like an angel anyway.

The way he loved her could almost make you jealous.

I have to find Claus, for him.

Fender is the only one who hasn't lied to me, who hasn't used me. All that time he was himself with me: angry and broken.

Lucas nods at me and I leave. I slip through the group of tourists to the stairs.

I know Lucas is close behind me, but I don't look back. Claus mustn't suspect anything.

On the second floor, I see a couple by the balustrade, watching Fender. I hear them saying how beautiful the song is.

There's a family with two young children, a business-man, a member of the hotel staff, and group of girlfriends in their forties.

Fender has half the hotel glued to his playing. A strange sense of pride comes over me.

I glance back. Lucas is hiding behind one of the plants. I can see a bit of his shirt.

He's not being very subtle.

I peer around the entire second story, but I don't see Claus anywhere.

Could he be waiting on another floor?

I flash Lucas a quick signal to stay here. I don't want to run the risk of him being seen.

I take the stairs to the third story, but it's completely empty. On the top story, there are more people. A little boy of about seven is hanging enthusiastically over the balustrade. His mom is holding him back, clinging to the tip of his hood.

No Claus.

Downstairs, Fender hits a wrong note. I realize that I'm holding my breath, but luckily he recovers quickly.

Where's Claus? Why isn't he keeping to the agreement?

I look at the big gold clock above the entrance. It's five past eight now.

I lean over the balustrade and make eye contact with Lucas. I shake my head and he signals at me to come back.

Maybe this was a test to see if we would do as we were told. Or maybe Claus saw Lucas after all.

What will the next message from Room Service say?

I nod at Lucas and go back to the stairs. Then I walk along to Room 311 and pause for a moment.

As Fender's music slowly dies away, I look at the gold numbers on the door.

Why did Claus choose that particular room? Sneaking me into a strange room was a huge risk, unless he knew no one was there at that point.

But how could he have known that?

I look at the little peephole in the wood. Every hotel room door has one.

The penny drops.

He could keep an eye on this room because he was in the room opposite!

At that moment, I feel a hand over my mouth and someone roughly pulls me backward.

Give him his due: Fender plays beautifully.
But I'm not going to be distracted.
I can see that he's following her.
Do they really think they'll get away with this?
They're not following the rules of the game.
I go back to my room.
Even in here I can hear the music.
It's time for a new plan.
If they don't make a sacrifice,
I'll choose someone myself.
But who?
The music stops.
I walk to the door.
When I open it, to my amazement,
I see Linnea standing there.
On her own.
As if she has come to offer herself up.
I grab her and pull her inside.
Finally the endgame has begun.
Let's see if the new girl *is* worth saving.

EVACUATION PLAN

FENDER

As I walk back to Kate, everyone congratulates me on my playing. There's applause from the balconies.

"Where's Linnea?" I ask.

"You did brilliantly," says Kate.

"Where is she?"

Lucas comes to stand with us. "It all went fine, but Claus wasn't there."

"Why aren't you with her?" My eyes flash to the stairs.

"She's coming," says Lucas. "Calm down."

I look up at the balconies, where the audience is slowly drifting away.

There's no sign of Linnea.

"I played a wrong note," I say.

Kate shakes her head. "No one noticed."

"You're making me nervous," says Lucas. "Chill a bit."

I look at the clock above the entrance. Ten past eight. Where is she?

My heart leaps when I see a blonde girl coming downstairs, but it's not her.

The seconds tick away.

"Let's go look in our room," says Kate. "Maybe she went there."

I was right. She doesn't like the look of this either. I follow Lucas and Kate.

Linnea must be in the room. She has to be. I bet she's sitting on the bed, her grin spreading across her face because she's just outsmarted Claus. She's probably found out his room number—the right one this time.

Maybe she's already making a plan to surprise him.

It's four against one. We have to win.

Kate opens the door. There's no one on the bed, but in the corner there's something big covered in a white sheet.

Kate puts her hands over her mouth. Lucas swears.

Linnea! That's the first thought that shoots through my mind.

I hurry over and take one corner of the sheet between my thumb and index finger. With a feeling of dread, I give it a tug.

But it isn't Linnea. It's the bear. Claus has brought it back.

First its paws emerge and then its stomach. Finally I pull the sheet off the head, which leans lopsided against the wall.

Then I'm startled as something black rises to the ceiling—a helium balloon tied to the bear's paw.

And that's when I see the damage. There are rips in the bear's head. Its white stuffing is bulging out. The biggest tear runs the entire width of its forehead.

It's lost an eye.

There's a card attached to the balloon, and I recognize Claus's handwriting.

An eye for an eye.

"No . . ." Kate's breath catches in her throat.

"Why?!" Lucas says, pounding the wall with his fist.

I look at the bear again, which looks back with one eye.

Claus has wounded the bear in exactly the same way she was injured last year.

An eye for an eye.

Claus has Linnea.

Too bad about the cute stuffed bear, though.

LINNEA

Where am I?

I feel nauseous.

There's a stabbing pain in my head.

I reach up to touch it.

Bad idea.

I groan.

"You were out of it for a while there. I even had time to run a little errand while you were asleep."

I recognize that voice, but who is it again?

"Here, drink up."

I feel a glass with something cold in it on my lips.

Don't drink it.

But I drink it anyway.

It's hard to swallow.

My head is pounding.

I try to open my eyes, but the light hurts.

Where am I?

"There, that's better." That voice again. "Take your time."

The name surfaces from somewhere inside my memory.

"Claus . . ."

"You got it," he says.

I remember the hand on my mouth and being pulled backward. I was out in the hallway when it happened.

Slowly I open my eyes wider, and the room starts to come into focus. And then I see Claus's face, less than two feet away from mine. There's a faint smile on his lips.

I have to get away. Now.

Why won't my arms work?

"Sorry." Claus nods at the headboard. "I had to take precautions."

I follow his gaze and see two ropes around my wrists. He's tied me up.

"I'd rather not, but it's for your own safety."

Panic overwhelms me. I start tugging like crazy on the ropes. They cut painfully into my wrists.

"Hey, hey, calm down." Claus tries to soothe me. "There's no point in struggling. You'll just hurt yourself."

My eyes shoot around the room. There are papers and envelopes all over—and a stack of those silver domes. There's some kind of plan hanging on the wall, but I can't make out what the writing says. Photos of Kate, Fender, and Lucas.

Claus really *is* Room Service. The evidence floods over me.

He seemed so nice, so decent. How can he have played a double role without me suspecting anything?

This is like the lair of a serial killer.

Is he actually going to murder me?

I think about the glass of water.

Why did I drink it?

I tug the ropes again.

"Hey, no." Claus puts a hand on my forehead and gently pushes me back onto the mattress. Under his hand I feel a blazing pain.

"You're bleeding," he says. "You have a head wound."

A head wound? So that's where the pain is coming from. What did he do to me?!

"Help!" My voice rasps and I cough. I have to shout louder. So loudly that the whole hotel can hear me.

I take a deep breath to try again, but then I feel Claus's hand on my mouth.

"Don't you dare." Claus's voice suddenly doesn't sound calm or friendly anymore. "If you scream, I'll have to hurt you again. And I don't want to do that."

I stare into his crazy eyes. Isolde must have been so afraid of him.

"So you'll keep your mouth shut?" he asks.

I can hardly even nod.

Claus slowly takes his hand away. "Great. Then we can finally talk."

FENDER

Kate isn't speaking. She's lying on our bed, facing away from me. I know she's crying, but I don't have the energy to comfort her.

Lucas is slumped, defeated, in one of the chairs, staring into space.

We left the bear in the room next door, but it still feels like it's here in front of me. The image is burnt into my memory.

An eye for an eye.

"Why did you leave her on her own?"

Lucas looks up. "Stop it."

"Stop what?"

"Stop blaming me. It's ridiculous."

"Really?" I arrange the messages from Room Service on the bed.

I keep rereading them, but I don't see any clues. Linnea could be anywhere.

"She trusted you. You said you'd protect her, and now she's gone. That creep took her."

"She wanted to do it on her own," Lucas says defensively. "You know how stubborn she is."

I think about it. Why didn't Linnea scream when Claus took her? There are hundreds of people in this hotel. Someone would have helped her.

Was she distracted?

I think about the moment when Linnea came back in from the courtyard. She was different, was acting strangely.

"She wasn't herself," I say. "What happened between the two of you outside?"

Lucas's face clouds over. "Here we go."

"Just tell me!"

"We kissed. That's all."

Kissed? Lucas? And Linnea? I try to picture it, but I can't.

"You don't need to look so surprised. I like her."

I can't help but burst out laughing. "You?"

Lucas has never liked anyone like that. He always said he wasn't interested in romantic stuff.

"Yes, me. What's wrong with that? She's nice. I know you can't stand her, but . . ."

No one hates something for no reason.

Except you hating me, right?

"That's not true," I say quickly.

"Yes, it is, and she feels the same way about you."

"Did she tell you that?"

Lucas nods. "Just this afternoon."

I'm shocked, but I don't really know why. It's not news that Linnea and I don't like each other, is it?

"She asked about Isolde too."

I look up in surprise. "What did you say?"

"That you two were the perfect couple, that she was really chaotic and a bit of a worrier. That was about it."

Spinner's got this.

"Did you mention her nickname?"

Lucas nods. "Is that not allowed or something?"

"But why did Linnea call herself Spinner?" As soon as I say the words, it hits.

Kate sits up. The last of her mascara has left a light-gray trail on her cheeks.

"Did you call Linnea that?" I ask, feeling bewildered.

Kate shakes her head, but her cheeks say something different.

"That nickname was hers." I stand up. "Is Linnea a replacement?"

I try to process it, but this is so . . . sick. I remember Kate's smile on the very first day of school this year. Was Linnea allowed to join our gang because she and Isolde looked like each other?

Then something occurs to me.

"Did you tell her to wear her hair in a braid too?"

There's silence. So it wasn't a coincidence that they both had braids. Linnea doesn't really look like her. Kate just made her that way.

I try to imagine how it must have felt for Linnea when Lucas told her about the nickname Spinner. It's hardly surprising that she wasn't herself. I'd lose it too if I found out I was a substitute for a dead friend.

"Y-you have gone completely insane," I stammer.

"What do you care?" says Kate. "You hate Linnea anyway!"

Lucas and Kate are right. I did hate her.

But something's changed. Maybe it happened when she fainted in my arms or when she lashed out at me.

When she was so angry, she seemed a lot like her.

Actually, I'm no better than Kate.

I liked Linnea only when I saw the resemblance to *her*. I made Linnea into a replacement too.

She sacrificed herself for friends she can't trust. We're wrapped up together in one big web of lies.

If anything happens to her now, it's my fault. Just like a year ago.

I wasn't able to save *her*, but it's not too late for Linnea.

I walk to the door and open it. No one asks where I'm going. No one asks what I'm going to do.

I slam the door behind me so hard that the echo booms along the hallway.

I have to find Linnea.

LINNEA

The church bells ring outside, but I lose count. How long have I been in here?

Claus is sitting on the edge of the bed. The ropes are cutting deeper and deeper into my wrists, as if someone has pulled them tight. My arms are cramping up. I'm exhausted.

"How much do you actually know about Isolde?" asks Claus.

"Not much."

"So your friends never told you anything about her?"

"They're not my friends. They're *her* friends. I was just allowed to borrow them for a while."

I don't want to say that, and certainly not to Claus, but then, to my surprise, I see his expression soften.

"What happened?" he asks. For a moment I see a glimpse of the boy I first met: considerate and understanding.

A thought shoots through my mind: *This is it. I have to get him on my side, make him feel some sympathy.* I remember a movie I watched not that long ago with my mom and dad. A kidnap victim got friendly with her abductor and was eventually able to escape when he left her unguarded.

New energy flows through me and I sit up straighter.

"Kate calls me Spinner. I didn't know it was actually Isolde's nickname. I thought Kate came up with it for me."

"That's disgusting," Claus says with a sigh. "And the braid was her idea too, I bet."

What? The braid? I remember Kate braiding my hair. Did Isolde wear her hair in a braid?

"Yeah, that was her idea," I say quietly. "I hate them. All three of them."

"Really?" asks Claus.

"Really." Have I gone too far? But Claus seems to be deep in thought. It's time to use my tactics.

I have to handle this like the girl in the movie.

"I know you don't want to do this," I say quietly. "You're not a bad person. You really helped me this afternoon. Thanks to you, I finally dared to stand up to Fender."

Claus nods slowly.

I start crying. I don't even have to try too hard. The tears weren't that far away.

"Stop it," he says quietly. "You know I can't handle it when girls cry."

"Sorry," I say as I splutter and start to cough. Before long, I really will have breathing problems.

"Stop it," says Claus.

"S-sorry," I pant.

"Calm down." I feel a hand on my head again, close to that painful wound. "Come on, calm down."

He gently strokes from my forehead to the start of my braid, his hand moving slowly along the herringbone pattern. His touch disgusts me, but I force myself to stay calm. I don't want him to suspect that this is all fake. I have to keep it up.

Claus's hand stops at the tip of my braid. I hold my breath. Is he finally going to untie me? If he does, then the door's not far. I can reach it before Claus realizes I'm making a run for it.

But then a sharp pain shoots through my skull, like my head's splitting in two. Claus has grabbed my braid and is pulling my head back. Through a haze of tears, I see Claus's face close to mine.

"Do you think I don't know what you're up to?" he hisses.

I try to shake my head, but immediately regret it. A new jolt of pain makes me gag.

"Wh-what do you mean?"

"You're trying to mess with me." Claus pulls my head back even more.

"No!" I scream. "I'm not! I'm not!"

"Do you think I'm stupid? Why would you kiss someone you hate?"

The kiss with Lucas. Claus saw us together.

"You're one of them, so that makes you just as bad." Claus pulls harder still. It feels like all my hair is coming away from my scalp.

"I'm sorry!"

"You really have no idea what happened that day." Claus's voice cracks.

"Then tell me," I plead.

Claus lets go of me and I fall back onto the bed.

Weeping, I close my eyes and pull my legs up. The ropes slice viciously into my skin when I roll onto my side, but anything is better than looking at him.

FENDER

I go downstairs and approach the receptionist.

"Excuse me, could I ask you something?"

"Of course. You played beautifully, by the way."

It takes me a moment to realize she's talking about my piano performance.

"Thank you. Um, I just wanted to ask if there's someone called Claus staying here. Could you maybe check the system?"

"I'm not allowed to do that."

"I wouldn't ask if it weren't really important."

The woman hesitates. Why won't she just do it? I drum my fingers on the counter. A new solo. When all of this is over, I'm going to work it out on my guitar, just for her. And a little bit for Linnea too.

"Please." All my despair is in that one word—and it works. The receptionist focuses on her screen. I hold my breath as she scans the guest list.

"Do you have a last name for him?"

"No," I say. "Just Claus."

After what seems to be an hour, the woman looks up.

"He's not here."

"What?"

"There's no one with that first name staying at the hotel right now."

I turn around.

"Sorry," I hear her say, but her voice sounds far away, like I'm swimming underwater.

I walk to the stairs and sink down onto the bottom step.

He checked in under a different name. He must have.

If I'd been quicker when Room Service called, I could have caught him.

I could blame Lucas and Kate, but I'm really the only one who's to blame.

An eye for an eye.

What if he does the same to Linnea as happened to *her* last year? I picture Linnea covered with scars.

That can't happen. It must not happen.

"Fender!" A slap on my back startles me. "What are you up to?"

It's Kate's dad. Frank's wearing khakis with a shirt and tie and carrying a folder with the logo of his law firm on it.

"Hey. I . . ."

"You guys have a good dinner?" Frank continues. "The desserts here are out of this world."

"Yes, sir. It was great," I manage to say. "Thank you."

"Sir?" Frank bursts out laughing. "Since when am I a *sir*?"

"Um, sorry," I say quickly. If I go on like this, I'll give myself away.

"Is everything okay?"

"Yes."

"And is my daughter having a good time?"

"Sure is." My voice sounds high and strained.

"I was going to come by to say hi this evening."

"No!" It just slips out. "I mean . . ."

"I get it." Frank puts his hand on my shoulder. "That's the last thing my teenage daughter wants, right? Yep, I know better than to burn my fingers on that one."

I force a smile.

"Have fun. Say hi to Kate and the others."

He has no idea that "the others" is just Lucas right now.

What would he do if I told him the truth?

For a moment I consider confessing everything. About Claus and the bear and Linnea.

But then I remember the rules of the game. The last time we ignored them, Claus took Linnea. Who knows what he'll do this time?

"Will do," I say.

Frank heads off to the restaurant. Thank goodness he's not going to come say hi. I don't even want to think about him seeing the room.

That's going to happen tomorrow anyway, but we're safe for now.

I know better than to burn my fingers on that one.

It's like all the cogs inside my head start turning at once.

That's it.

Fire.

LINNEA

"Why are you lying to me?" Claus paces the room. "If you do that, I'll have to hurt you again."

My head feels like there are a thousand needles jabbing into it. I turn my face even more away from him.

Why did that Isolde ever get involved with him? He is seriously disturbed.

"You have no idea how hard it was to arrange all this. I needed a room on the same floor as yours—and it costs a fortune! So you're not going to spoil this for me. You hear me? Those so-called friends of yours need to be punished, if it's the last thing I do."

"Why?" I stammer. "Why are you doing this?"

"Someone has to." Claus is still pacing up and down. "They murdered her."

I shake my head. "It was suicide."

"Is that right? If a gang of people breaks you down until you can see no other way out, is that suicide?"

I think about the diary.

"But she hated you too."

I can tell right away that I've gone too far. Claus falls silent. And then there's a huge bang. The champagne bottle has smashed into the wall beside the window. Pieces of glass fly everywhere, and a puddle of champagne spreads over the carpet.

"I *loved* her!" Claus shrieks. "More than that Fender ever did."

I cringe. I can't stand up to him again. It's way too dangerous.

"He didn't deserve her." Claus wipes the bubbles of spit from his mouth. "He murdered her."

"How . . . how did you get her diary?"

I have to keep Claus talking. It won't be long before he realizes he can't imprison me here forever. And who knows what he'll do to me then?

Claus straightens his back. "There was a memorial service at her house. I walked right in. I think her mom and dad were really happy to have someone there who said he was a friend of hers. While her brother was giving a speech, I went to Isolde's room. Her diary was still under her pillow."

He stole from her bedroom while her family was mourning. What kind of person does that?

I'm silent, but my face must show my disgust, because Claus walks over to me and says, "I'm not proud of it, if that's what you're thinking, but someone had to do it. Those three can't be allowed to get away with it. Isolde's death needs revenge."

"Then what am I doing here?" I force myself to look at him. "What's your plan?"

"You'll have to wait and see," says Claus. "I'm only just getting started."

FENDER

My hand hovers over the button. I know what's going to happen. Last year, some joker set off the fire alarm at school for fun.

Within ten minutes, everyone, including the teachers and the janitor, was outside in the schoolyard.

There's a hefty fine for the inappropriate use of the alarm, but I have to do this.

Linnea has to be found.

I push the red button.

For one second, it's silent, but then the alarm starts shrieking. The sound penetrates every fiber of my body.

I flatten myself against the wall and watch as the doors to the rooms open one by one.

I just hope I have the right floor. It was a guess, but he must be somewhere close to us. Right up at the top.

More and more guests are coming out. Men, women, children. Big, small, long hair, short hair . . .

"Come on, Claus," I say quietly. "Where are you?"

≏

The sound is deafening.
I open the door a crack and peep through.
The whole hotel is emptying out.
I take a step into the hallway.
"Out of the way!"
A woman pushes me aside and hurries past.
"There's a fire!" someone shouts.
A fire?
There's no way I can escape
with Linnea without being seen.
Has this all just been a waste of time?
At the end of the hallway,
a boy is leaning against the wall.
He's the only one who's not headed outside.
Our eyes meet and linger for a couple of seconds.
It's Fender.

FENDER

He's here.

Claus is exactly as Linnea described him: a boy you'd hardly notice, unless you know who you're looking for.

Before I can blink, he's disappeared.

"No need for concern," I hear someone from the hotel calling down the hallway. "Please proceed calmly outside. Take the stairs."

I sprint to the other end of the hallway. The door Claus came out of is closed. When I see the gold numbers, I gasp.

Room 312.

Opposite the door that Linnea and I knocked on.

We were so close.

I try the handle, but of course it doesn't work.

"Open up!" I pound the door as hard as I can. Should I smash it down, like I've seen people do in the movies?

"Claus, I know you're in there. Linnea! Linnea, is everything okay?"

My voice cracks. A few last guests walk past me.

"Young man!" The hotel employee shouts down the hallway. "Everyone has to leave the building."

I bang the door again. "Claus, open up. Now."

"Young man!" The man comes hurrying toward me. "Do you hear me?"

"Claus," I say. "Please . . ."

Then something is slid under the door. I look at the gold envelope at my feet.

Without thinking about it, I snatch it off the floor and put it in my inside pocket.

The man from the hotel is standing beside me now.

"Outside. Now. This is not a drill."

I look at the door. If I go, I'll be leaving Linnea with that madman. But if I tell this man that someone's being held captive in there, Claus could panic. What if it makes him do something to Linnea?

My only choice is to go with the man.

"I'll be back," I say quietly as I walk down the hallway. "I promise."

When I get outside, there are hundreds of people on the sidewalk. Amid all the commotion, I hear someone call my name and I see Kate making her way over to me through the crowd.

"Fender! Where were you? I was so scared that you . . ."

"There is no fire," I say. "It was me who set off the alarm."

"Why?" Lucas comes over to join us.

"To force Claus out of his hiding place." I look back at the Riverside. "He's in Room 312."

Kate's eyes widen. "You've seen him?"

"Yes, he came out when the alarm went off, but he closed the door when he saw me." I take the envelope out of my pocket.

"He pushed this under the door for me."

I take a folded sheet of paper from the envelope. Kate gasps—she recognized it immediately too.

She used the same speckled paper last year for the invitations to her party. The invitation hung on my bulletin board for a week.

Later that week I pulled it down and tore it into a hundred pieces. I kept ripping away until tiny scraps were all that remained. It looked like it had been snowing in my bedroom.

"Read it," stammers Kate.

INVITATION

Congratulations!
You have been invited to the party of the year.
Wear your finery and come to Room 312 at 11 p.m.
At midnight on the dot we'll drink to a wonderful new
*   year of life.*

Claus

181

"Kate . . ." She has the same despair in her eyes as I feel inside.

Was this what Claus wanted all along? Is that why he took Linnea? So he could be certain we'd show up?

"Okay, people. Everyone back inside," shouts a hotel employee. The rest of his words disappear inside my crowded head.

Around us, the sidewalk is slowly emptying, but we stay there.

I've found Linnea, but she feels more out of reach than ever.

All the messages from Room Service were nothing. They were just a warm-up for the grand finale: Kate's birthday.

LINNEA

He was here. Fender was here, but he went away.

He left me behind.

"W-we have to go," I stammer. "There's a fire. . . ."

"There is no fire," Claus snaps. "It was that friend of yours."

The wailing alarm stops as suddenly as it started. The echo rings inside my head.

It takes a moment for my ears to get used to the silence, but then I can hear the usual sounds again.

There are lots of voices out on the sidewalk, like people standing in line for a concert. And then I hear one voice above all the others.

"Okay, people. Everyone back inside. It was a false alarm. Someone pressed the button just for fun. We'll find out who it was. On behalf of the Riverside, I offer my sincere apologies for the inconvenience."

Claus was right. There is no fire. Could it really be true that Fender pressed the button? But why?

Claus pulls one of his suitcases out from under the bed. He has a few of them, as if he's packed for a year.

I notice that my muscles automatically tense up.

I'm only just getting started.

What was Claus talking about? What's he planning?

I move my wrists back and forth. There's a little play in the right one.

If I'm careful, Claus won't notice. And if I get one hand free, I can free the other.

"Hey!"

The blood freezes in my veins.

"No funny business." Claus looks at me threateningly. "Got it?"

I nod, my breath racing.

"Great. Then I'll get it all ready." Claus bends over his suitcase again.

Get it all ready? What does he mean? A shiver runs down my spine.

Where are Fender and the others? Maybe they'll just abandon me to my fate.

"Okay." Claus stands up. He's holding something black. "Sorry, but I want you to have the same surprise as your friends."

Before I can protest, Claus pulls a trash bag over my head.

FENDER

The bathroom mirror shows a version of me that I don't recognize. My pupils are dilated, like I've been living on coffee for days. I've pulled my hair into a tight bun again.

"Ready." I leave the bathroom and look at Lucas, who is lying on our bed. He's unbuttoned his shirt, and his hair is a mess.

"Why didn't you get ready?"

Lucas sits up. "I'm not taking part in this."

"You have to."

"I don't have to do anything. I'm done with this. Screw that Claus guy. I'm not following his orders."

I can hardly believe what he's saying.

"What about Linnea? This isn't a game, Lucas!"

"I know that!" Lucas comes to face me. "You don't need to keep repeating it."

"If you like her as much as you claim, you wouldn't say that."

Lucas's expression hardens. "Take it back."

"It's true, though, isn't it?"

We've never argued before, let alone physically fought, but it feels inevitable now.

Lucas takes a step forward so our noses are almost touching. I see the face I know so well. At camp we woke up like this every morning in the tent, almost lying on each other's mats.

"Linnea deserves better than someone who'll abandon her."

Lucas's eyebrows shoot up. "Since when do you care about Linnea?"

I turn around. "I just don't want Claus to win."

"You said just now that it isn't a game." Lucas takes me by the shoulder and turns me back to face him. "Why are you so keen to save Linnea?"

Another image from last year flashes through my mind. What if this all ends the same as it did then?

"Just get yourself ready."

The door opens and Kate appears. She's wearing a little floaty black dress. It comes to just above her knees and flares out at the bottom.

It makes her look older, but at the same time really vulnerable. Her bare arms are crossed over her body.

"Can someone help me with the zipper?" She looks at me. "I can't quite reach it."

I nod. When Kate turns around, I take hold of the silver zipper. I want to tell her I'm sorry, that I never meant to hurt her. That I'll make sure everything turns out okay this time, that she won't lose another friend.

But the words stick in my throat.

I look at the birthmarks all over her back. Kate hates them, but *she* thought they were great. One big beauty spot, that's what *she* called it, and since then Kate has hated them a bit less.

I do up the zipper.

"There you go," I say.

"Thanks." Kate turns around. "I actually brought this along for tomorrow. To celebrate my birthday. Not for . . ."

She glances at Lucas.

"Are you going to get ready?"

Thankfully Lucas doesn't protest again, but buttons up the shirt. "We need to take a weapon."

Kate shakes her head. "What are you planning to do? Stab Claus?"

"Of course not, but we'd be mad to go in there unarmed." Lucas looks at me for backup. "Right?"

I think about Claus. At the end of the hallway, he looked smaller than I'd imagined.

He was even a bit nerdy, in those glasses of his.

"No, we're not doing that," I say. "He'll search us. If we take any weapons, he'll go wild."

A church bell rings. I count the number of chimes.

Eleven.

"We stick together," says Kate, looking at me, then Lucas, and back at me again. "Whatever happens, we stick together."

LINNEA

I can hardly get any air with this trash bag over my head. Every time I breathe, I suck it into my mouth. My top lip is wet.

I'm going to suffocate.

This is just like in the lift that time. There's no escape.

I want you to have the same surprise as your friends.

What was Claus talking about? What is he doing? I've heard him moving around for a few minutes now, but I have no idea what's happening.

To keep calm, I focus on my right hand, which is getting looser and looser. Meanwhile I listen closely to see if Claus is nearby.

As long as I can hear Claus moving around, I'm safe.

I hear a familiar tune. Claus is whistling cheerfully, as if this is one big party.

What if I don't get away?

What if I die here?

I start breathing faster, pulling the bag deeper and deeper into my mouth.

The plastic tastes bitter.

What will my mom and dad do when they hear what's happened?

Will they ever get over this?

I think about Isolde's parents. Their daughter has committed suicide. All they have left of her is that suicide note. But soon my parents will have nothing.

I'm going to die with a trash bag over my head.

No.

That is not going to happen.

I have to keep fighting.

I wring my hand back and forth again, and the rope suddenly comes free, like a ring stuck on your finger when you soap it up and pull.

Claus stops whistling. I quickly grab the rope so it looks like I'm still tied up.

Footsteps head my way.

"Let's take a look."

His voice makes me shiver. Claus is suddenly really close. I smell strong aftershave, which he must have just put on.

He leans over me. Is this the moment to attack? But it's two hands against one, two eyes against none.

Claus checks my left hand and gives the ropes a quick tug.

He's going to find out what I've done.

In my head, I count the seconds.

Any moment now . . .

There are three loud knocks.

"Coming!" Claus's voice is loud beside my ear.

"It's your friends," I hear him say. "Are you ready to party?"

Then he yanks the trash bag off my head.

FENDER

I'll count to ten, and if he hasn't opened the door by then, I'm knocking it down.

One.

Two.

Three.

Four.

The door swings open. In front of us is the boy I saw in the hallway.

Perfectly ordinary.

Black hair.

Black glasses.

Green eyes.

Not handsome.

Not ugly.

The boy next door.

What did she see in him?

"You're on time. Good." Claus steps aside and beckons us in. "Come on, guys."

Lucas stands there, frozen. Kate hesitates. I'm the first to react.

"Where is Linnea?" I hiss.

"She's inside. Calm down. She's fine."

I step into the room. The first thing I see is the coffee table, covered with a tablecloth with three silver domes on it. The sight of those things practically makes me gag.

There are candles everywhere, as if this is some kind of romantic dinner.

Linnea is lying on the bed. The girl I hated so much for taking *her* place, for being alive when *she* was not.

Linnea's hands are tied to the bedposts. There is a bright-red gash on her forehead, with blood trickling from it. It's dried, but it looks bad.

"She isn't fine at all!" I try to go to her, but Claus stops me.

"Stay here."

How dare he hurt Linnea? That Room Service stuff was bad enough, but she has absolutely nothing to do with this.

The way she's lying there, completely defenseless and terrified. Has he gone completely mad?

I'll beat him to a pulp. I'll kill him.

I raise my fist to take a swing at him, but then I crumple. A shock runs through me, which I feel from the top of my head to my toes.

Lucas swears. Kate screams.

I fall to the floor, twitching. It's like I've lost all control over my body.

What *is* this?

"What did you do?" wails Kate.

"It's a stun gun," says Claus. "Don't worry. It's not lethal. Just really painful."

I try to get up, but my muscles won't cooperate. I lie on the carpet, gasping for air.

"So are you going to listen now? Or would you rather I give Linnea a turn?"

I'd rather die than listen to him, but I know he has all the power here.

"S-sorry," stammers Kate. "We'll listen to you."

They all stare at the stun gun.
Did they really think I'd be unprepared?
I've had it for weeks.
Ordered it online, didn't even need a permit.

LINNEA

Lucas shoots forward and helps Fender to his feet. When Fender stands up, his eyes meet mine for a moment.

I can read all kinds of emotions in his eyes, but what's he thinking?

Then he gives me a little nod.

I nod back.

It's no more than that.

We don't dare to do any more.

"Sit down." Claus points at the cushions on the floor around the coffee table. "I made a seating arrangement."

When no one reacts, Claus tuts.

"If you want me to let Linnea go, you'd better listen."

It works. Fender and Kate sit down beside each other, with Lucas opposite, and Claus at the head of the table. He still has his stun gun in his hand. It's a weird yellow thing that looks like a pistol, but with two pins at the end of the barrel instead of a hole. I saw what it did to Fender. Claus said it's not lethal, but I'm not so sure about that. If you held it to a body for long enough . . .

Claus nods at the champagne cooler. "Time for a little drink."

When no one reacts, Claus continues.

"How did you like my invitation? Was it a bit like last year's?"

So that was what he slipped under the door when Fender was here. This is what it's been about all along: Kate's birthday. Does he want to relive last year? I look at all the candles around us. In another situation, this setting would have been beautiful, but now it's just terrifying.

"I thought it might be a fun start to the party if we tell Linnea what happened last year."

I'm startled by the sound of my name. Is he serious?

"She knows *nothing* about it," says Claus, feigning shock. "That's a bit sad, isn't it?"

No one says anything; everyone stares ahead, as if paralyzed.

"Well, then I guess I'll just tell her myself."

"No." Kate interrupts him. "I'll tell her."

She glances at me. I can see she regrets everything, but there's no time now to forgive her.

"Everything went wrong on my birthday last year." Kate's voice trembles a bit. "Isolde got hurt and . . ."

"No, no." Claus raises his hand. "You *will* start at the beginning, won't you?"

Kate looks at Lucas and Fender for help. "But this is what matters to you, isn't it?"

"The *whole* story, please." Claus taps the first silver dome with his finger. "Start with this one."

Does he have more messages for us? I hold my breath as Kate lifts the first dome.

There is a gold envelope under it, which Kate opens. It has the same paper inside as before, with ragged edges and a picture of a mouse on it.

Another excerpt from Isolde's diary.

I clench my right hand around the rope. When the moment comes, I'll have to be quick. Very quick.

I have to get out of here alive.

Kate's eyes shoot along the lines. "Do I really have to read this out loud?"

Claus nods. "We're listening."

When Fender plays, I forget almost everything.
Almost.
Because Claus sticks around, always.
Look at Kate and Lucas happily singing along. They
        don't have a care in the world.
Sometimes I feel lonelier when I'm with them than
        when I'm alone.
What if I tell Fender the truth?
Maybe he'll get so mad at me that he won't even hear
        what I want to tell him.
Then I'll have lost him for good.

Kate's voice is so shaky that she has to stop for a moment. I look at Fender, who is twisting his hands together. I can see that all he really wants to do is attack Claus again, but I can only hope that he controls himself.

*I needed to pee, so I went into the bushes, not that far
from the campfire.*
I could still hear Fender playing from there.
When I found a spot to go, I looked around.
Maybe I was being paranoid, but I had to be certain.
As soon as I started to pee, I heard rustling.
It was really close.
I stood up before I'd finished.
I had to get out of there as quickly as possible
"Isolde?"
It was him.
*"Claus?" My heartbeat was practically audible. "What
are you doing here?"*
*"I just came to take a look." He pointed at the place
where our campfire was. "Having fun?"*
I didn't want to answer, but nodded anyway.
*"You don't look happy." He took a step closer. "I can see
there's something wrong."*
You're here, I wanted to say, but I didn't do it.
"I don't feel too good."
*"You're lonely." He reached out his hand and stroked
my braid. When he reached the tip, he gave it a
little tug. "I can see that you're lonely."*

He was right—and he knew it. But it was because of
  him. And I think he knew that too. Maybe that
  was why he kept coming to see me. The more often
  we saw each other, the more secrets I had from the
  others. Claus was gradually isolating me. I was
  transforming from a country into a peninsula. And
  eventually I would become an island.
"Kiss me."
I looked at him. Was he serious?
Claus leaned forward and pressed his lips to mine. His
  hand clawed under my braid.
I wanted to push him away, but my body froze. I could
  only wait for him to stop.

"You . . ." I'm startled by Fender's icy voice.

Kate is just in time. She grabs Fender by his jacket and
pulls him back into his seat.

"Don't do that," she says quietly. "Think about it."

FENDER

Claus was there that night.

He put his hands on her.

While I was playing a song in blissful ignorance, Claus was groping her.

He kissed her.

Why didn't she call me? I really would have listened to her. I always listened, didn't I?

"You assaulted her."

I don't care anymore that Claus will give me a shock. My blood is boiling.

"Keep reading," Claus says to Kate. "Then everything will become clear."

I'm in the hospital for the first time in my life.
Pain all over, but I have to write.
Or I'll forget what happened.
The paper has to remember it for me.

When I got back to the campfire, Kate was lying with
     her head on Lucas's shoulder. Fender put his guitar

down and rested his head on my lap. I ran my
fingers through his curls. I loved it when he wore
his hair loose instead of in a bun. He gave me a big
smile.
I had to tell him the truth, that night.
Lucas looked at me over the fire. Did he know what
I was thinking? I felt like I was caught in a trap.
"Want to do something fun?" I asked.
Fender opened his eyes and looked at me lazily.
"Like what?"
Kate stood up. "I have an idea."

The ruin in the woods must have been empty for years.
The building was like a skeleton without any flesh
on the bones.
Our flashlights shined from left to right like a sort of
light show.
"Creepy," said Fender.
"Magical," I said.
The inside of the building was in even worse shape
than the outside. The stairs to the upper story were
rickety and creaky.
But I kept going. I wanted to get rid of Claus's touch,
and the adrenaline worked like a kind of shower.
When I reached the top of the stairs, I gasped for
breath. The floor up there had collapsed. There
was just one long beam running from one side of

the room to the other. If I put one foot off the beam,
I'd plunge down below. But I could see the stars
through the holes in the roof.
I grabbed the bottle of wine that Kate was holding and
took a few big gulps. I didn't actually like it, and the
alcohol made me dizzy.
"Come here." I pulled Fender toward me and kissed
him.
I didn't care that we had an audience.
"What did I do to deserve that?" asked Fender when
I finally released him. My lipstick was around his
mouth.
It felt like it was our last kiss.
Like I knew what was going to happen.

I remember that moment.

Our last kiss . . . For me, it felt like the first. I remember being certain at that moment that I wanted to grow old with her.

How could I have been so dumb?

"I challenge you," said Kate as we looked at the beam.
"Walk over to the other side without falling."
"If you make it, I'll write a song for you." Fender
removed any remaining doubt.
It was pitch dark on either side of the beam.
You couldn't even see the floor below.

"Don't do it." Lucas stopped me. *"You're really drunk.*
You're going to fall."
"I'll do what I like." The words came out in bumps and
jolts, like I was going along a bumpy road. "So long."
I put my right foot on the beam.
"She's really going to do it!" Kate cheered me on.
When I was halfway across the beam, I glanced up
for a moment. The starry sky was so glorious that
it made me cry. Why was everything so incredibly
broken?
"Isolde?"
I heard Fender's voice and looked back.

Then.
That was when I said her name.
For the last time.

I lost my balance. That must have been it, because I
was suddenly falling.

Why did I call her? What exactly was so very important
right at that moment?
No matter how many hours I've spent worrying about
that question, I still can't remember.

I heard voices shouting all at once. Footsteps coming
closer.

"An ambulance!" Kate shouted. "We need an
ambulance. Lucas? Lucas!"

There was no answer.

"Hang in there!" said a voice. "Please, hang in there."

It was Fender.

I looked and saw his sweet eyes, full of panic.

There was no need for him to be afraid. I was okay.

Maybe the stars would calm him down.

"Look," I said to him, pointing up. "My star sign."

But then the pain hit me like a tidal wave.

I flailed at my face.

"Take them away! Take these knives out of my face!"

Now I realize that it was glass.

Thousands of shards of glass.

I'd fallen on a sheet of glass, face down.

Like diving into a swimming pool off the high board.

A silence falls.
The end is approaching.
I can't wait.
Finally they're listening.
All of them.

LINNEA

"Fender, the next one is for you."

It doesn't seem to worry Claus that Fender is having to listen to his girlfriend's experience of that night of horror.

"Fender can't . . ." Kate looks at Claus. "Let me read it."

Claus shakes his head. "No, that's against the rules."

"Screw your rules!"

Kate stands up and throws her dome across the room. It bounces off the bathroom door and rolls under the four-poster bed.

"Sit down." Claus raises his stun gun. Does Kate really want to make him mad? Could she be that dumb?

"What do you want from us?" Kate throws her arms in the air. "Money? Maybe we can arrange something with my father. He's a lawyer. He makes loads of money. I'm sure I can get him to—"

"Sit down," says Claus again, putting his finger on the trigger. "And don't insult me."

Kate's eyes shoot fire. For a moment I'm afraid she'll attack him, but then she sinks back into her seat.

"Okay, the next dome, then." Claus looks at his watch. "We'll have to hurry a bit or we'll miss twelve o'clock."

He's really enjoying this.

I see that Kate is doing everything in her power not to explode at him.

Fender picks up the silver dome and takes the envelope from underneath. Every movement seems to be an effort, as if he's hurting all over.

I touch the rope on the left with my right hand. Now I can feel that there's a double knot in it. How am I ever going to untie it?

Pain.
That's what I remember from the ambulance
ride.
Excruciating pain.
I wanted to die.
But in the hospital they fought for me.
For my face.
I slept through it all.

The rope begins to loosen. I can move my left hand just a little bit more—and then more.

If Claus looks this way now, the game is up.

But he only has eyes for Fender, who collapses more with each word.

The dressings are finally off.
Today they let me look in the mirror.
They say it's me.
But all I saw was a monster.

My hand is so painful, but I keep frantically trying to pull the rope free. I have to get out of here alive.

Mom and Dad say it's not that bad.
Even Marius is going along with it.
He says I'll always be his beautiful little sister.
But as he was saying it, he couldn't even look at me.

"Why did you stop?"

I'm startled by Claus's voice. Fender has lowered the diary pages and tears are streaming down his cheeks.

I've never seen him cry before.

"Keep reading."

"No." Fender shakes his head.

"You will keep on reading. Now!"

"No."

"All right." Claus pulls the pages from his hand. "Then I'll read it."

Fender came by today.
I heard a nurse in the corridor tell him he had to
understand that I'd changed.

"Changed." That truly is what she said.

Like I'd dyed my hair.

Or was wearing different clothes.

She didn't mention my eye.

Or the volcanic eruption that was my face.

I wanted to shout that Fender should stay out there
in the corridor, but he was already coming into the
room.

I dived under the covers.

"It's me," he said.

"I know."

"Will you come here? I want to hold you."

"No, you don't."

"Of course I do. It's us."

I wanted to believe him so badly that I came out from
under the covers.

I heard him gasp.

It was just a very small intake of breath.

Minuscule.

But big enough.

FENDER

"That's not true," I manage to say. "That's not what it says."

"That *is* what it says." Claus fixes his gaze on me. "You were disgusted by her."

"No. Absolutely not." I search for the right words. "I . . ."

Claus's eyes narrow. "You had the shock of your life when you saw her."

"Go away," I said.

Fender didn't leave.

Instead, he just stared at me.

I thought it was so bad, how everyone avoided looking at me, but this was way worse.

"Let me hold you."

"No." I put my hands over my face. The face I would have to make do with for the rest of my life. One functioning eye, dozens of scars.

And lots more operations ahead to make it bearable.

I was no longer the girl he'd fallen in love with.

Not even a tenth of that.

"Go away!" I screamed. "Go away, go away, go away!"
I kept shouting until my throat was raw. And even then
    I kept going. I emptied out my entire body.
After what seemed like hours, I felt two hands on my
    wrists.
"Hey, hey, calm down."
I was looking into a nurse's face.
Fender had listened to me. He'd gone.

I climbed out of bed and looked around the corner of
    the door.
They were standing nearby.
Kate and Fender, by the coffee machine.
The two of them entwined.
Finally she could hold him like that.
She must have been waiting for that all her life.

LINNEA

"This is ridiculous." Kate shakes her head. "She's acting like I was happy and—"

"You were," Claus cuts her off. "Admit it. You have everything you want, except for one thing. Or should I say: one person?"

Kate's eyes are filled with blind panic, as if she's about to lose everything.

"Fender, don't listen to him, it's not true."

But Fender doesn't seem to hear her. He's just staring straight ahead.

"We're almost there," Claus continues. "The last one's for you, Lucas."

Claus just keeps on going, like a bulldozer crushing everyone in his path.

"I'm not doing this anymore," says Lucas.

"What?"

"You can read it out yourself." Lucas looks up. "Give me ten electric shocks if you like, but I quit."

I hold my breath. What's he doing? We've all seen what Claus is capable of.

"In fact, we're leaving." Lucas stands up and looks at Fender and Kate. "You guys coming?"

Claus jumps to his feet and reaches me in two strides. He presses the stun gun to my temple.

"You're going to leave Linnea with me?"

"Leave her alone."

"I know what I said about it not being lethal, but if I use it in this spot, that might be a different story. So what's it going to be? Running away—or Linnea?"

I feel the pins pricking my skin. What would it feel like to get a shock?

"Well?" Claus presses the weapon deeper into my skin. "You really like her, don't you?"

Lucas raises his hand as a sign for him to stop. "Okay, okay. I'll read it."

Today I went back to where I used to live.
I had to see them one more time.
Kate, Fender, and Lucas were sitting in the schoolyard,
    in our usual place.
There was another girl with them.
A blond girl, like me.
A girl with a flawless face, like I once had.
I have no idea who she is.
Lucas said something funny. Fender laughed. Kate was
    kind of clinging to him.
As I stood there watching, it suddenly hit me.

They've moved on without me.
While I'm just going backward.

I feel the pain in every word that Lucas reads out. I don't dare look at Fender.

Claus is sitting on the edge of the bed, with his back to me. The rope is getting looser and looser. Any minute now, my left hand will be free too.

Claus must have spotted me, because he came after
*   me. Close to the station, he caught up with me and*
*   grabbed hold of my wrist.*
"Isolde?" He was out of breath from running. "Is it
*   really you?"*
I could have denied it, but my identity is written ten
*   times all over my face. Even with operation after*
*   operation I'll still look like this.*
"What are you doing here? Ah, it doesn't matter, you're
*   here now."*
He held out his hand and took my sunglasses off my
*   face.*
He stared at my scars and then stroked them with his
*   index finger. He kept stroking the biggest scar in*
*   particular, the one on my forehead.*
I felt tears burning in my eyes.
"Don't do that," I said.
"Why not?"

"You disgust me."

Claus sneered at me.

All the contempt in the world was in that one look.

"I disgust you? Think yourself lucky that anyone wants to touch you at all."

FENDER

I don't even think about it.

With a yell of rage, I throw myself upon Claus, hitting him wherever I can. We roll onto the floor, right next to the bed.

"How could you dare to say that to her?" I thump him in the ribs.

Claus holds the stun gun to my shoulder. "Want some more?"

I'm no match for that thing, no matter how much I want to fight. I lower my fists and roll off Claus.

"You just don't get it," I pant. "She meant everything to me. She still does! What happened to her destroys me every day."

I forget that Linnea, Kate, and Lucas can hear everything.

"Don't you understand? I was the one who called her name. It's my fault that she fell. She lay there in a pool of her own blood, and she pointed up at the stars. And then she mumbled something about star signs. I think, even at that moment, she was trying to comfort me."

I can barely swallow away the lump in my throat. I'm almost choking on my own words.

"If I could, I'd take on all of her pain. I didn't think she was ugly or scary—anything but."

"You gasped when you saw her," shouts Claus. "That's what it says in her diary!"

"Of course I was shocked. It was my fault that she looked like that. They weren't able to save her eye. She'd never be able to see with it again."

I take a deep breath.

"I couldn't find her in the place she'd moved to. I waited at the harbor every Friday, but she never came."

"You're lying," says Claus.

"No, I'm not. I've never forgiven myself, and I never will. That's why I couldn't look at her. Not because she disgusted me, but because I felt so guilty. I haven't said her name ever since that night."

For a moment, there's silence.

I can see that Claus is completely stunned. In the few seconds it takes him to recover, I dive forward. Before he can react, I snatch the stun gun from his hand.

I grab his shirt and hold the stun gun to his temple. It's not lethal, he said, but what will happen if I do this?

"You're no better than I am," I hiss. "We both destroyed her."

"Fender," I hear Kate say. "Please, let's call the police. They can take him away."

219

"No," I growl. "I want to do this myself."

If only she were here now, then she could have seen me taking on Claus. She could have told me everything, and I would have helped her.

"You still don't get it, do you?" Claus looks at me. His voice suddenly sounds different. "You still don't get who I am."

What's he talking about? Is he trying to buy time by playing some new game?

"You're a psychopath. That's what I get."

I put my finger on the trigger, but just as I'm about to pull it, someone yanks back my arm.

"Don't do it." It's Linnea, who's freed herself from the ropes. "Listen."

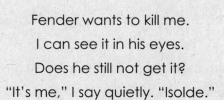

Fender wants to kill me.

I can see it in his eyes.

Does he still not get it?

"It's me," I say quietly. "Isolde."

LINNEA

"It's me," I hear Claus say in a voice that sounds softer than before. Girlish. "Isolde."

I feel Fender's muscles tensing. I don't know if I can still hold him. He's staring at Claus as if he's possessed.

"Kate," I shout.

Kate finally starts moving and gently takes the weapon from Fender's hand.

"It's me," Claus says again. "Don't you recognize my voice?"

He stands up.

I look at the boy in front of me. The boy with the average face. I've talked to him. I'm one hundred percent certain he's not a girl.

"That's not possible," Kate stammers. "Isolde's dead."

Claus shakes his head. "I really wanted to do it, but I couldn't."

"But . . . we saw the death notice. We got the suicide note . . ." Kate sounds like she's about to faint.

"I placed my own death notice in this morning's newspaper. I left the house before my dad could read the newspaper. I posted the suicide note myself."

Kate shakes her head. "You can't be Isolde. You're lying."

"You're the one who's lying, Kate. You're all lying." Claus grabs his own hair and pulls. For a moment I think he wants to hurt himself, but then his black hair comes away from his head.

I gasp for breath as blond strands of hair appear from under the wig. And finally: a braid.

"It's a disguise." Isolde drops the black wig by her side. "I didn't want you to know it was me. Do you know something? I've stood by the train tracks dozens of times because I wanted to jump. I've stood in the bathroom with a razor blade in my hand, and I've lain in bed with a bottle of sleeping pills. I wanted to die, because of you guys. I wanted to make you feel what it would be like if I really had dared to do it."

I stare at the boy in front of me. It's Claus, but it's also Isolde. It's too much to handle.

"I was so happy when *you* suddenly appeared outside the door," Isolde says to me. "My replacement. If I mutilated you, they'd have to go through everything again. And your life would be over, just like mine is. I've been practically dead for a year. The Isolde from before has been murdered. But I can't do it. Seems there's still a bit of the old Isolde left inside me after all."

"B-but why . . . ," I stutter. "Why did you disguise yourself as the boy you hated? I mean, you wrote about Claus and . . . Did you make him up?"

"No, he's not made up. But he's not really called Claus. That's an alias."

I touch the wound on my head. This is all one big nightmare.

"So what's his name?"

Isolde looks at me. "Did he hold your braid too when you kissed?"

None of this makes sense. "What?"

"The alias," says Isolde. "Claus. Shuffle those letters."

Shuffle the letters? What's she talking about?

"Lucas," comes a voice from the floor. Fender is still staring straight ahead. "If you rearrange Claus, you get Lucas."

CHECKOUT

FENDER

Claus and Lucas are the same person.

Claus was an anagram for the biggest secret she was carrying around. There was no way she could use Lucas's real name, so he became Claus.

She made Lucas into a character, as she often did with strangers.

She's so very good at it.

She could become a writer.

I look at the boy with the blond braid in front of me.

This can't be her.

She's dead.

"Lucas is your best friend. You would never have believed me." She rests a hand on my arm, but I pull it away.

This is too much.

I can't do this.

When I turn around, I see that Lucas has disappeared. Where's he gone?

I jump to my feet and head into the hallway. Someone calls my name, but I ignore it. I'll talk to Lucas first. I need to hear this from *him*.

I look left and then right. At the end of the hallway, I see someone darting around the corner.

I run down the hallway. Ahead, a door with a red-and-white sign on it is clattering. The emergency exit. Lucas is escaping onto the roof.

The stairs up there are steep. With every step, Claus's words echo through my mind.

It's me.

Claus is Lucas.

C L A U S = L U C A S

At the top of the stairs, I fling the door open, and the wind blasts into my face. For a moment, I'm overcome by the darkness outside, but then I see dozens of lights from the buildings around me.

"Lucas!" He is standing right by the edge, looking down. "What are you doing?"

Lucas looks around. "Stay there, Fender."

"Please step away from the edge."

"I said stay there!"

"Okay, okay. Calm down."

Lucas looks down again. His feet are just a couple of inches from the edge. My shirt flaps around my body.

"Lucas, listen to me," I say quietly. I think about how Linnea found me this afternoon on the windowsill. She calmed me down by talking to me. As long as we're talking, Lucas can't jump.

"I know it's not true. There's no way you can be Claus."

The wind carries my words away. Did he hear me?

"You're my best friend, aren't you?"

Down below, car horns are hooting. I can hear an ambulance nearby, as if they're already on their way.

Then Lucas starts laughing. It's high-pitched and shrill. "Is that what you think?"

He slowly turns around.

"Do you really think we're friends?"

I shake my head. "This isn't the time for jokes."

"I already knew Isolde before she came to our school. Did you actually know that?"

What's Lucas talking about? I take a step forward.

"We met at camp. For days, all we did was kiss. I was really upset when we had to go home. Little did I know that two weeks later she'd step into our classroom."

What is he talking about? All three of us saw her for the first time that day. I remember the moment well. I immediately had the feeling that I was walking more upright, as if someone had put a string on the crown of my head and pulled upward.

"That first day, I took her aside and kissed her, but she didn't want to anymore. The day after that I tried again, but then she told me that I liked her more than she liked me."

Lucas has gone crazy. He's making this up. He has to be.

I'd have noticed if there was something going on between Lucas and her. They were right under my nose every day!

"And then she started to like you. I could see it happening, but I couldn't stop it. I didn't want it to get out of hand like that, but she didn't understand. She thought the two of you belonged together."

"We did," I say.

"You did not!" Lucas screams. "What we had was real. I've never felt that way about a girl before!"

His words make me dizzy.

"I couldn't look at the two of you. You were touching someone who belonged to me."

"But she was *my* girlfriend," I stammer. "Not yours."

I look at him. Lucas inches backward. His heels touch the edge of the roof.

"You had everything and I had nothing. Kate is head over heels in love with you, but you never even noticed. Linnea was the first one not to fall for you. In fact, she hates you."

Is that why Lucas kissed her? I shake my head.

"Please step away from the edge."

"Why should I?" Lucas moves back a little more. His heels are over the edge now. One gust of wind and he'll fall.

"It's all over, Fender. When I saw that wrecked room, I already had a suspicion that Isolde was behind it. And when I heard the name Claus, I was sure of it. She wanted to punish me for what I'd done. And she involved you guys because it's our fault she got mutilated."

"But it wasn't like that!"

"We murdered her, that's how it feels to her. She's insane."

"Don't talk like that about her." I take two steps forward.

"Stupid Fender, are you still in love with her? After all these months? Even now that you know I had her first?"

I look at the boy opposite me. Is this the same Lucas I woke up next to at camp? The boy who dragged me through the hardest time ever?

All I really want to do is turn around and walk away, but at the same time I know I'll never see him again if I do. I never want to have that feeling again.

He deserves to be punished, but not like this.

Even Linnea rescued me from the window, although she hated me.

In a reflex, I reach out my hand and grab Lucas. With a sharp tug, I pull him away from the edge and we fall backward together onto the roof.

The gravel jabs into my body and I feel Lucas's weight on top of me.

It's over.

REVIEW

LINNEA

Isolde hasn't moved. She's been sitting on the floor this whole time, with the wig in her hand.

Kate and I stare at her, without saying anything.

Fender and Lucas are sitting out in the hallway, a few feet away from each other. They haven't said anything about what exactly happened between them, but I can guess.

I'm mainly happy they're both back, even though the thought that Lucas kissed me makes me nauseous. I was an Isolde replacement for him as well. The girl with the blue eyes and the blond braid.

Kate reaches for my hand and entwines her fingers with mine. I want to pull my hand away, but I leave it there.

This is not the time for a fight.

"Linnea van der Zee?" Kate and I are both startled by a voice behind us. When we turn around, we see two police officers.

"Yes, that's me."

"You're the one who called us?" The male officer looks at us. "Can you explain exactly what happened?"

I look over at Isolde. The edge of her mask is visible where her real hairline begins.

How did she disguise herself so well? There's no sign of her scars or her damaged eye.

But more important: how did she manage to identify so closely with a character who was based on the person who started all this misery?

Claus seemed completely real.

At least for a while.

"No," I say quietly. "I can't."

<hr />

"Let's go to the station to continue our discussion." The female officer looks at Isolde. "Your parents are going straight there."

We just told the officers everything, but Fender had to keep stopping because it became too much for him. Kate and I took over from him then. We worked together like a well-oiled machine.

Isolde starts moving. Throughout the whole story, she's been staring at Lucas, but he hasn't even glanced back at her.

I look at Isolde again. Part of her mask has come loose now and is hanging from her face like a piece of meat. Underneath, I can see some of her scars emerging. She has removed her green contact lenses. Her one good eye is blue. That's another similarity between us.

The male officer points at the stairs. "Our fellow officers are taking care of the other parents downstairs. Maybe it's a good idea for you guys to wait down there too."

My mom and dad . . . When I was in Claus's room with that trash bag over my head, I thought about them. And what it would be like if I didn't survive.

How am I ever going to explain to them everything that happened here? When we told the whole story to the officers, it was like I was talking about someone else.

How can anyone ever understand how I felt?

In the lobby, I look up at the gold clock above the entrance one last time. The hands show that it's long past twelve.

It's now officially Kate's birthday.

One year later.

I look at the signs around the edge.

"What is Isolde's star sign?"

Kate looks at me in surprise. "Libra, why?"

I breathe a sigh of relief. Not Capricorn, thank goodness.

"Kate?" The voice of Kate's father booms around the lobby. "What's going on? Why are the police here?"

Frank puts his arms around his daughter and hugs her tight.

I look at them for a moment, then head outside. The doorman tips his hat as I walk past.

If only I could turn back time to yesterday. When Lucas was still just Lucas, and Claus was no more than a plan in Isolde's head.

We were going to have a great weekend, with great food and swimming in the dark. After all, you can see the stars through the glass dome.

I drop down onto the edge of the sidewalk and sigh deeply.

Behind me, I hear a voice.

"Can I come sit with you?"

FENDER

"Can I come sit with you?"

Linnea looks up at me. "Why would you want to do that?" Her voice sounds muffled, as if she's under a silver dome.

"I was looking for the only honest person here."

Linnea nods. "Sit down."

We sit in silence, but this time it's not bad. We have nothing to say to each other. Or maybe too much.

The officers come out, with her between them. She glances in my direction. Her mask is coming off, and I recognize every line in her face.

How many times have I thought about what it would be like to see her again?

It never went like this.

In my mind, I see her running along the jetty. She loses her sneakers, but still goes on running. Stumbling, just to get to me as quickly as possible. She joins me in our hiding place, and the two of us make characters out of the people in the harbor.

Now she's being led away by a police officer, toward his car. I look at the officer. What could his name be? Probably something short. John, or Bob, or something like that. I bet he has a dog. One of those yellow Labradors, which stinks when it's been for a swim.

"Why are you smiling?" asks Linnea.

I look up. "I wasn't."

"Yes, you were."

Maybe Linnea's right, although there's certainly no reason to smile. I'm exhausted, but we still have so many hoops to jump through.

My parents are sure to have a hundred questions. Not to mention *her* parents. Have Tom and Jeannette spotted the death notice placed by their daughter, who is still very much alive?

I gaze up the sky. The stars aren't nearly as impressive as they were last year, but still I see the same constellations.

Look, my star sign.

She was comforting me at the moment when it should have been the other way around.

I cup my hands around my mouth and, for the first time in a year, I shout her name.

"Isolde!"

GUESTBOOK

The five-star hotel in the city where I used to live was always a part of Amsterdam that was out of reach.

What would it be like to sleep there?

With that question in mind, I started writing.

That's the great thing about making up stories: you get to go to places that are normally off-limits.

When I was writing this book, someone I know also gave me a tour of a five-star hotel. Thanks to Lilian, Riverside suddenly took shape!

I'm just not sure I'd ever dare to spend the night at a five-star hotel.

Because I'm far too scared that I'd be sitting in one of those luxurious rooms and suddenly there'd be a knock at the door.

"Who's there?" I'd ask.

And the answer would be: "Room Service!"

—*Maren Stoffels*

Don't miss another un-put-downable thriller from Maren Stoffels.

I can see It from here.
It can't see me.
It has to pay.
For everything.
All I need is a sign.
Please.
Give me a sign that I can begin.

MINT

"He's gay. For sure." Sky's sitting on the backrest of the bench, right behind Alissa and me. It's just the three of us. The rest of the park is deserted.

"Don't think so." Alissa takes out her wallet. "How much do you want to bet?"

I have no idea who my two best friends are talking about. Their conversations often pass me by, like I'm on the other side of a wall.

Alissa waves a five-dollar bill around. It reminds me of the first day of junior high. I thought Alissa had made a bet then too.

She came up to my desk that first morning and asked if the seat next to me was taken. Alissa was the kind of girl who could have sat anywhere. She was so incredibly beautiful. Her eyes were the color of the sea on the Italian coast, where I'd spent the summer. I looked around suspiciously. Where were her giggling friends, laughing at me from a distance because I'd fallen for it?

But there was no one else there. We were the only ones in the classroom.

Sky's voice brings me back to the present. "Let's bet for a pizza," he says. "And Miles can deliver it. Perfect."

So they're talking about Miles, who works at the pizzeria with Sky. I've never seen him before, but Alissa's mentioned him a few times.

A girl with blond hair and a red scarf around her neck comes jogging into the park. As she passes us, she flashes me a quick smile.

"He's on his way, so now we just have to wait and see." Sky puts his phone in his pocket and casually rolls a cigarette. He never has actual packs of cigarettes. Sky always does everything just a little bit differently from everyone else.

"Did it hurt?" I hear Alissa ask. I'm back on the bench in the park. What were they talking about now?

I follow Alissa's gaze to Sky's eyebrow piercing, which he had done a while ago. When he turned up at school the next day, the skin around the piercing was red and swollen. I touch my own eyebrow, which also hurt for a few days.

At first I thought it was a coincidence, but then when Alissa broke her wrist in gym, mine was painful for weeks too.

Can I feel other people's pain? Is that possible? It feels supernatural, weird. And if anyone finds out, I'll get even more of a reputation for being crazy.

Sky points at his eyebrow. "So much gunk came out! I could have made it into a smoothie."

Alissa gives him a shove and he nearly falls off the back of the bench. "Stop! You're going to scare me out of it."

Since when has Alissa wanted a piercing? I try to imagine what it would look like on her, a little ring through her eyebrow.

A couple weeks ago in Textile Studies, we had to make

dresses out of garbage bags. Alissa pulled hers over her head, grabbed hold of it on one side, and shot a staple through the plastic. Then she paraded around the classroom like she was on a catwalk. Some of the boys started whistling. Even in a garbage bag, she was stunning.

"Where's that pizza?" Alissa asks impatiently.

"Miles has half an hour to get here. After that, the pizza's free."

A few minutes later, a scooter with a big blue trunk on the back drives into the park.

Sky grabs my wrist and looks at my watch. "Bang on time. Typical Miles. You see? He's a punctual gay guy."

My stomach's churning, like I'm about to take an important exam.

"Stop it." Alissa quickly straightens her T-shirt. It's a small gesture, but I can tell she's nervous.

Miles brakes in front of our bench and gives Sky a wave. When he lifts the visor of his helmet, I see two bright-blue eyes, like Alissa's. But there's something cold about these eyes. They have nothing to do with the Italian sea, but are more like icy water. I get a weird feeling that I can't quite identify.

"One pepperoni pizza?" The boy takes out a pizza box. The scent of melted cheese makes my mouth water.

"Yep. It's for us." Then Sky points at Alissa. "She's paying."

"You think?" Alissa looks at the boy. "Hey, Miles."

MILES

I don't like it when people know my name and I don't know theirs. Feels like I'm down 1–0.

I've seen this girl before. She meets Sky after work sometimes. I noticed her immediately because she has the same blue eyes as me. Dad used to say I was the only one except him with blue peepers like this, but he was wrong. This girl's eyes are hypnotic.

Did Sky tell her my name?

The girl smiles. "Want a slice?"

I hesitate, because I really need to get going, but something about her voice makes me stop.

It's only then that I notice the other girl on the bench. She's leaning forward slightly, with her straight hair hanging over her face like two curtains. She doesn't quite seem to belong.

"It's almost time for your break, isn't it? Come on, have some." Seems the girl with the blue eyes knows not just my name, but my work schedule too.

I can see part of her bare neck.

What would it feel like to kiss that soft bit of skin?

I'm startled by my own thought. After Karla, I made up my mind never to feel anything for a girl again. It's easier to reject them all than to let anyone get close. Because when they get close, they start asking questions. Questions I can't answer.

I know I should go, but somehow I find myself taking off my helmet and sitting down beside her.

"Here." The pretty girl passes me the box. As I eat my slice, I dare to sneak a closer look at her. There has to be something about her that's disappointing, something that'll help me to forget about her later.

But her voice sounds like she's singing. Her eyes are an endless blue. And she smells like autumn sunshine.

I'm not sure I want to forget her.

I swallow the pizza. "And who are you?"

ALISSA

We're sitting so close that Miles's leg is touching mine. He's looking at me as if he hopes to find something in my face. His eyes scan every inch of my skin.

I've never talked to Miles, but whenever I go to meet Sky at work, I watch him from a distance.

Miles stands out, not because he's good-looking, but because he doesn't seem to want to be. It's as if his looks torment him somehow. And that's something I recognize.

Boys like to check me out, and it drives me crazy. Andreas is the last boy I kissed, and I really did like him. But after our kiss, I heard him bragging about it like I wasn't even a person, just some "hot" girl.

Sky's handsome too, but his rough-and-tough exterior scares a lot of people off. Which seems like a great idea to me.

At home, I sometimes stare at myself in the mirror. I don't dare get a tattoo, but how about a piercing? Once I put a dot on the side of my nose with a Sharpie. The thought of a stud in my nose instantly made me feel stronger.

"And who are you?" asks Miles.

"Alissa."

"Are you gay?" Sky asks.

I get why the teachers say he's direct. He's like a bulldozer sometimes.

Miles shakes his head irritably. "No, I'm not gay."

Sky lights his cigarette. "No need to get pissed. Gay people are cool."

Miles puts the last bit of pizza into his mouth and stands up. "Got to go."

Is he leaving because Sky asked that question? I realize that I'm riled up. I want Miles to look at me again the way he just did. It was like he could see much more than my exterior.

"Sky's paying for the pizza," I say. "And the tip."

SKY

I curse to myself.

Alissa likes him.

I thought this was just about a bet, but Alissa smiled at Miles the way only she can. Her boy-slaying smile.

When I get home, I turn the amp for my electric drum kit up high. Drumming always works, but not this time. Even after playing for half an hour, I still feel angry. I pull off my head-phones.

Why can't I shake it off?

Alissa doesn't have a clue that I only started dating Caitlin to divert attention.

Caitlin's in our year at school. If I squint, they even look a bit like each other. But Caitlin's blue eyes don't match up to the real thing.

I fall back onto my bed and look at the group photo on my nightstand. Having it there makes it hard for me to sleep, but it's even harder without it.

I pick up the photo and hold it close to my face. There's a small worn patch where I sometimes press my lips to it. We're standing close together, our arms touching.

I'd really like to cut everyone else out of the photo, but this way Alissa can come into my room without realizing what's up. There's no need to worry about Mint. She spends half her time floating in another dimension.

"You belong with me," I say quietly to the photo. "You just need to see it."

MILES

Alissa. Every pizza I deliver for the rest of the evening, I'm thinking about her. As I ride my scooter home, I can still see her bare neck.

I don't realize where I am until I'm almost at the front door. This is my old street.

How is that possible? All this time, I've never gone the wrong way. I settled into our new place immediately.

My heart skips a beat when I see that nothing's changed. The sidewalk is lower in one place, where I could always ride over it on my bike without bumping the back wheel.

In the window of number 39, there's still a line of wooden cows on the ledge. I used to spend ages looking at them when I was a little kid. Dad stood patiently beside me as I counted them and gave them all names.

The memory's painful.

Nothing's changed here, and yet *everything* has changed.

SKY

On Friday afternoon, I'm happy when I can finally leave school. I know I shouldn't be mad at Alissa, but I still am.

She's in love with the wrong person. Why can't she see that?

I head into the employees-only section at the pizzeria and, as I'm putting on my apron, I spot a flyer on the table.

Curious, I read the words.

SUPER-REALISTIC ESCAPE ROOM!
THE HAPPY FAMILY

THE DOOR SHUTS.
YOU HAVE SIXTY MINUTES.
BUT WHERE WILL YOU START LOOKING?

FIND THE CLUES! CRACK THE CODES! SOLVE THE PUZZLES!
CAN YOU ESCAPE WITHIN AN HOUR?

BUT BE WARNED:
THIS IS NERVE-RACKING, BLOOD-CHILLING, HEART-STOPPING!
NOT FOR THE FAINT OF HEART OR THE FEEBLE OF BRAIN!

THE HAPPY FAMILY IS DESIGNED FOR GROUPS OF AT LEAST 4 PEOPLE.
(THIS ESCAPE ROOM IS TERRIFYINGLY TENSE!)

I read the flyer three times to let it all sink in. The word "super-realistic" has sucked me in. I always think the haunted houses at the county fair are ridiculously fake, but this? This is something I have to do.

Maybe, just maybe, just for a moment, I'll forget the photo on my nightstand when I'm in this Escape Room. And maybe I'll forget that those blue eyes will never look at me the way I want them to.

"Shouldn't you be working?"

I turn around and see Miles. He points at the flyer in my hand. "What's that?"

I'm mad at him too, maybe even more than I am at Alissa. Those longing looks he was giving her yesterday. I just can't bring myself to look at Caitlin that way, no matter how hard I try.

I stuff the flyer into my jeans pocket. "Nothing."

Alissa and Mint are waiting outside when I leave work later. Alissa's piercing twinkles away at me. Like she wasn't pretty enough already.

"You coming to the movie?" Alissa asks.

"Got a date with Caitlin." The moment I say it, I feel nervous again. Recently I've had the feeling that Caitlin wants to go further than just kissing. I know I should want the same, but I can't do it. My mind's on someone else.

"Things are pretty serious with you two, huh?"

I make a strange noise that could mean anything. A quick change of subject.

"Want to go here next Friday?" I pull the flyer for the Escape Room out of my pocket.

Alissa frowns. "What is it?"

"Oh, I've heard about that!" To my surprise, Mint pulls the leaflet out of my hand. "You have to solve puzzles so you can escape."

"And that's your idea of fun?" Alissa raises an eyebrow.

Mint nods. "Sounds cool."

Alissa exchanges a quick glance with me. She's clearly thinking the same thing I am: Mint's too timid to do anything. She usually stays at home when we have a school trip, and Alissa and I go to the fair on our own every year because Mint says the rides make her nauseous. She rarely visits me at work, always claiming she has a stomachache or headache.

"Fine by me," Alissa says.

I point to the bottom half of the flyer. "We just need a fourth person."

"Caitlin?" Mint suggests.

Being with Caitlin already feels like one big real-life Escape Room.

"Or Miles?" Alissa says.

I curse to myself. No way I want to spend sixty minutes watching those two getting closer.

"Then there'll be four of us." Alissa looks at me. "Shall I ask him?"